W9-CCP-334

Shadows in the Mirror

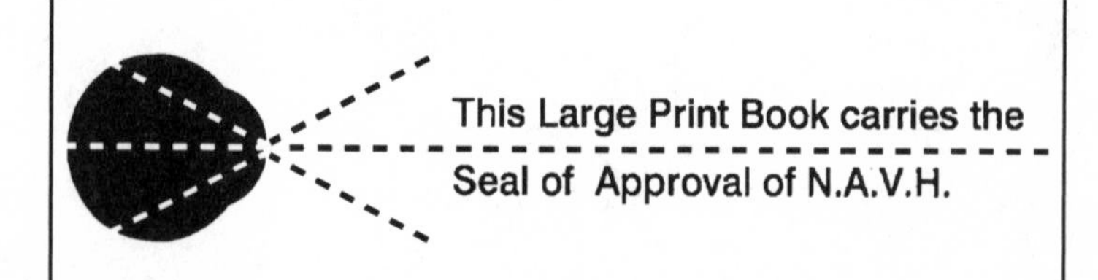
This Large Print Book carries the
Seal of Approval of N.A.V.H.

SHADOWS IN THE MIRROR

LINDA HALL

THORNDIKE PRESS
A part of Gale, Cengage Learning

GALE
CENGAGE Learning™

Detroit • New York • San Francisco • New Haven, Conn • Waterville, Maine • London

This is a work of fiction. Names, characters, places, and incidents are either the product of the author's imagination or are used fictitiously, and any resemblance to actual persons, living or dead, business establishments, events, or locales is entirely coincidental.

Thorndike Press® Large Print Christian Mystery.
The text of this Large Print edition is unabridged.
Other aspects of the book may vary from the original edition.
Set in 16 pt. Plantin.
Printed on permanent paper.

LIBRARY OF CONGRESS CATALOGING-IN-PUBLICATION DATA

Hall, Linda, 1950–
Shadows in the mirror / by Linda Hall.
p. cm. — (Thorndike Press large print Christian mystery)
ISBN-13: 978-1-4104-0662-0 (alk. paper)
ISBN-10: 1-4104-0662-8 (alk. paper)
1. Orphans — Fiction. 2. Parents — Identification — Fiction.
3. Large type books. I. Title.
PS3558.A3698S53 2008
813'.54—dc22 2008002792

Published in 2008 by arrangement with Harlequin Books S.A.

Printed in the United States of America
1 2 3 4 5 6 7 12 11 10 09 08

Lord, you have been our dwelling place
throughout all generations.
— *Psalms* 90:1

My Domino Diva writing buddies,
without whose support I'd never have
ventured into writing romance.
You gals rock!

Prologue

The little girl with the purple ribbons in her hair held tightly to the man's hand. He was taking her to the place of mirrors, he said. And the mirrors were the best place for playing. She would run in and out, between them and behind them and make funny faces. She'd stick out her tongue, and laugh and laugh. Then she'd sit on the floor and undo her purple ribbons and press them flat against the mirror. Sometimes Mommy leaned the mirror back and when she did that it made their faces look all funny and fat like plates or really skinny like crayons.

If she got up really, really close, her nose got big. And the way she got her nose to look even fatter was to squish it up against the mirror until it looked like a pig nose. When she breathed hard it left a dark place on the mirror that she could draw lines on with her finger.

But the man told her not to do that. It

smudges the mirrors. It makes the mirrors no good. And he would take a handkerchief out of his pocket and back and forth, back and forth, he would wipe them clean. But Mommy never minded when she wrote with her fingers on the mirror. Sometimes Mommy would take her up in her arms and they'd twirl in bare feet around the mirrors and laugh at their reflections, while Daddy looked on and smiled. Then he would open his arms and they'd both go into that special and safe place.

Before the man came for her that day, the little girl had been in the living room where everyone was quietly sitting on chairs. Mommy and Daddy weren't there.

"Where's Mommy?" The little girl looked around her.

"Child," someone said.

"You poor, poor thing." A lady she didn't know but who smelled like mashed potatoes ran her hand through the little girl's hair.

"Such a poor, poor thing."

The little girl sat down on the floor, her coloring books spread out all around her. She would wait for Mommy.

"Such a shame," someone said. "She doesn't understand, poor thing. She doesn't know."

"How can she know? She's too young."

"Such an honest to goodness tragedy."

"An orphan at such a young age. It doesn't bear thinking about."

The little girl had gotten up from her coloring and followed Scrapples the cat into the kitchen, and the man was there. He bent down to her level and put his fingers to his lips. He told her quietly that he was going to take her to the place of mirrors where she could be happy again.

"Is Mommy there?"

"Yes, of course. Mommy and Daddy both, and if you come now you can be with them forever." And he smiled at her.

She had to hold his hand tightly, very, very tightly and walk outside with him. Could she promise to do that? Could she keep a secret? She nodded solemnly.

He gave her a cookie and they walked out the back door, and no one saw them leave. It was raining.

Later, much later, they would ask her how it was that she had wandered out here and ended up asleep at the bottom of the root cellar. It was the cat, they said, that alerted them, the crying of the cat from the bottom of the root cellar. But how had she managed to open the heavy door all by herself?

They would wrap her up in a blanket and give her hot chocolate at the table and cluck their tongues.

"Poor child. So cold."

"Such a cold, cold day."

"Poor thing followed the cat outside."

"And clear down to the root cellar. But how had the hatch been up?"

They shrugged and looked amongst themselves. But on this strange and awful day, someone, they reasoned, had gone down for a can of peaches and left it open distractedly. Anything was possible on a day like today.

And no one thought to ask the little girl.

One

23 Years Later

"Mom, Dad," I whispered. "Things are good here. I want you to know that. I'm even sort of happy. The shop is doing well and I found a nice church to go to and I'm making a few friends. And there's even this guy who smiles at me."

Why did I just say that? I'm not ready for *any* man to smile at me. Especially not after the fiasco of my engagement. "Of course, you know my doubts because I've told you all of this in great detail, but it's still nice to know that I've still got it, whatever 'it' is. And in a couple of minutes, I'm heading downstairs for my class. I can't believe eleven people signed up for my mirrors class. I think you'd be proud of me."

I sighed and placed the framed photo of my parents back down on my end table. I let my fingers glide along the top and rest there for a moment. The thing was, I had no idea whether they would be proud of me or not. I don't know my parents. They were killed in a car accident when I was three and a half. All I have is this one picture. And yes, I talk to it. It's one of my quirkier habits, but it's one that gives me a strange sort of comfort.

"Hey, Marylee, hi."

I gasped, turned. Johanna, my best friend, or as best a friend can be after only half a year of knowing someone, was standing in my bedroom doorway. I stood up and straightened the photo on my nightstand.

She said, "Your door was unlocked." She motioned toward my kitchen and to the door that led out of my apartment and down the back stairs. "So I came in. I knocked on the doorjamb. Guess you didn't hear me."

She saw the look on my face. "Sorry. I should've knocked louder. I didn't mean to startle you. You were on the phone?"

"No." I offered no explanation. Not a lot of people know that I regularly talk to my dead parents.

She was still in the doorway, nervously urging one side of her hair up into a small jeweled barrette while she talked. "Oh, I can't get this — sorry for barging in — does this look all right?"

"You look fine." I moved away from the picture. "Your hair is beautiful." And it was. My friend always looks fine; petite and pretty.

"It's a hopeless frizz mop in this weather," she said. "Call me Medusa lady. Snakes for hair." My friend Johanna teaches English lit at the community college so she regularly peppers her conversations with literary references.

"No, your hair has body," I said, fiddling with her barrette. "Not like my straight mop. It rains and mine flattens into my head. And it's such a boring brown."

"You could get highlights. Your smiling coffee guy might like it." She was grinning and I was grinning and I was happy she was my friend.

"I don't have a smiling coffee guy," I said.

"Sure you do." She pointed at me. "The guy you keep telling me about, the one who just *happens* to be in the coffee shop every morning when you just *happen* to get your coffee, the guy who just *happens* to smile when he sees you, that guy." She reached into her pocket for her lipstick. Johanna never carries a purse; instead all of her jackets and pants have copious pockets in which she keeps loose change and lipsticks and combs and barrettes.

"He winked at me today," I told her.

"He winked at you!" She stopped and turned, holding the lipstick tube. "That's a step up from smiling, you know."

"There's no step up. There's no steps anywhere in a relationship that's not a relationship. I don't even know his name." I pulled my own hair back into a pink scrunchie I'd had on my wrist. "And besides, I'm not interested."

I wish I were glamorous. Or at least sort of pretty. But every time I look at myself I think of my aunt Rose who raised me; capable, smart, talented, plain. When I was fourteen a neighbor of ours called me *handsome.* That's me, *handsome.* No wonder my former fiancé dropped me like a sack of composted turnips.

"You need to learn the way things work, Marylee," Johanna said, capping her lipstick tube. "First there's the look, and then there's the half smile. You know, the mouth only up on one side." She did a pretty good facsimile.

"Then there's the full smile. And then there's the wink. And need I mention that your coffee guy is way beyond my Evan? I went into his photo shop today to get some pictures developed. All he said was, 'Hello, Johanna. Nice weather, isn't it?' That was it.

That was all. Nothing. After all we shared, he's talking about the weather."

"Johanna." I turned to her. "You're such a great person, you shouldn't be wasting your time on some idiot who's treated you horribly."

"He didn't treat me that horribly. He just never called me again."

"Same difference," I said.

I had heard often about the wonderful and famous Evan and the two glorious dates they'd gone on, and then how Evan hadn't called. Still, Johanna had multiple excuses for him. He was busy with work. He'd just come off a broken engagement. He'd been so hurt in life he had trouble committing.

She opened her mouth to say something and then clamped it shut and shrugged. Finally she said, "I just wish that someone, I don't even care who, would finally break through that thick hedge of his soul."

I grinned at her. "Oh, you *do* care," I said. "You want that person to be you. Admit it."

She put up both hands in mock surrender and shook her head. "No, I'm an adult. Seriously. I mean, of course I would like it to be me, but I'm ready for whatever." Then she added, "I pray for him every day, you know."

"Personally, I think you're wasting your time."

She shrugged, looked away from me. Were we good enough friends for me to say that to her? I hoped I hadn't hurt her, but it maddened me that my new friend was enamored of a guy who took her out twice and then just stopped calling with no explanation.

"Well," I said and pulled on my blue sweater, "we should get downstairs. Class awaits."

But she was standing there, quiet. "Marylee, may I ask who *were* you talking to when I came in? Did I interrupt something?"

Maybe Johanna could be trusted with some of the secrets of my life. "I was talking to my parents."

"Your parents!" She looked at me, wide-eyed. "On the phone? But, I thought . . ."

"I know it's strange, but I have a picture of them and I've been talking to that picture for, like, my whole life. It sort of, I don't know, gives me comfort. Sounds weird."

"It doesn't sound weird at all. Can I see them? Do we have time?"

I went and got the photo from the nightstand and showed it to her. She studied it. "She's so pretty. Your mother."

I nodded. In the twenty years since my

aunt Rose had given me this framed photo on my birthday, I had memorized every nuance, every shadow, every square inch. My father is handsome and tall and stands with his arm protectively around my mother. She looks up at him, her sweep of long blond hair falling gently down her shoulders to her waist. She wears a green cotton dress and is barefoot. They're both barefoot. Her feet are dainty and small, so unlike my own. She's young and pretty, younger than I am now. Behind them is the blue of Lake Champlain.

All of my growing up years I wanted hair like my mother's, long and softly curling and blond. Instead, mine is more like my aunt Rose's, plain and straight and brown. Plus, my mother is so slender, and I'm always battling five pounds, sometimes winning, sometimes losing.

Johanna looked at the picture and said, "I thought your mother was the picture you have in your living room, that one on the wall. The resemblance is quite strong. I always thought you look so much like her."

"No," I said. "That's my aunt Rose. She raised me after my parents were killed."

Johanna set the picture down on the kitchen table, where we now stood, and I made sure the French doors to the balcony off my kitchen were locked. I closed the curtains on the windows that overlooked the tiny porch. Actually, it was this little postage stamp of a wrought-iron deck that sold me on the place. It's only big enough to hold not much more than my wicker rocking chair, and even though it overlooks a back alley, I like sitting out here on warm nights with a book.

Doors, windows securely shut and locked, I grabbed my keys and said, "We better get going. Downstairs we have eleven ladies wanting to learn how to make mirror mosaics."

I armed the security system to my small apartment and we headed down the back steps to the craft shop I owned. I owned! I still couldn't get my mind around the fact that I'd owned Crafts and More for seven months now. A month ago I was even flush enough to hire a woman to work with me three afternoons a week. Barbara was a wonderful crafter who was using the extra money to help her youngest son who was in his first year in computer management at the Community College of Vermont, the same place Johanna taught English lit. I knew her from church where she led a weekday-morning crafts-and-Bible study. She bought lots from my shop. When I'd asked if she wanted to work here part-time, she'd said, "Sure! Why not? I'm here the equivalent of that time anyway."

I'd also begun offering craft classes in the community. My favorite was a scrapbooking class for seniors over at the Champlain Seniors' Center. In addition to tonight's mirror arts class, I had a quilting class. Plus, I had plenty more classes in the planning stages.

Johanna was wearing two different colored socks I noticed, as we headed back down the stairs. I smiled to myself. Johanna was good for me. My funky friend brought a lightness to my life that had been absent for too long.

Three women were waiting under the awning at the locked front door. "Hello, ladies," I said cheerfully, letting them in. "There's a bit of time, so if you want, you can pop over next door and grab a coffee. They're still open for a few more minutes. We won't start without you." I poked my head outside and looked through the large glass windows into the brightly lit coffee shop. But of course the man who got his coffee the same time I did each morning wouldn't be there. What was I thinking? And why was I even looking for him?

I was about to turn back when I saw

something. Or felt something. It was as if a dark hand had waved across the coffee shop windows. It disappeared so quickly that I couldn't get a handle on it, couldn't figure it out. A person? A cloud? Fog? What?

I held my sweater closed at my throat, but the sense of something, or someone, there made me quiver. I thought of my aunt's constant premonitions, her asking me to make a promise before she died. "Don't go back to Vermont. Whatever you do, don't ever go back to Vermont, Marylee. Promise me this!"

And I had looked at her skeletal face, wasted by the cancer that would take her in a matter of weeks, and made no such promise. Instead, I'd wept as I'd smoothed a wet cloth on the forehead of my mother's sister, the woman who'd raised me.

A chill so profound started at the tip of my toes and ended in a place near my forehead. I closed my eyes briefly.

"Are you okay?" A woman with gray curls approached me.

"Just a chill. It's cold out there," I said.

"Do you think so?" said someone else overhearing the tail end of our conversation.

"Warm for this time of year," said another from across the room.

"Supposed to rain," said someone else.

And while the ladies talked on about the weather, I drew back into my cheerful shop and made my way to the craft table in the rear. Earlier I had set out pieces of mirror, both glass and plastic. At each place I'd laid a nine-by-twelve mirror. I'd instructed the ladies to bring photos or pictures from magazines that they wanted to use in their mosaics. For those who hadn't brought pictures, I had a stack of old tourist magazines featuring scenes from Vermont and other parts of New England they could cut pages from. I had told them this was going to be a fun class and that anybody could do it. Even Johanna, who claimed she couldn't draw a straight line with a ruler, was going to participate.

Two more ladies entered; another two went for coffee and a few more sat down at the table and fingered through pieces of mirror.

"I've done decoupage, but never with mirrors," one said.

"It's something I learned from my aunt," I said with forced cheerfulness. I was still reeling from what I'd seen out there. Or hadn't seen. "But watch your fingers. Some of those pieces are sharp. We don't need any cut fingers tonight."

Ten minutes later all eleven women had arrived. Most of them seemed to know each other already. I had us fill out colored name tags with marking pens, but this was obviously more for my benefit than theirs. I stood at the head of a long table and began to explain mirror mosaic art as taught to me by Aunt Rose.

"Is it like tole painting?" asked a woman whose name tag read Gladys.

"Not really," I explained. "It's a bit like decoupage. But not exactly. It a bit dif—" I stopped. I began choking, coughing. I put my hand to my throat. My eyes went wide. I couldn't breathe. One of the ladies reached into her purse and handed me a paper-wrapped cough candy. "Thank you," I managed to say. I tried unwrapping it, but my fingers refused to find the edges of the wrapper.

This wasn't an ordinary tickle in my throat. A woman named Beryl was smoothing out the picture she'd brought with her. It was the same exact picture I had kept in the frame on my nightstand for all of my growing-up years. It was the picture that had listened to all my whispered prayers and thoughts. It was the picture I had said goodnight to almost every night of my life, and the one I had said good morning to when I woke up. I was still coughing. I needed to sit. I needed to flee. I needed to throw up. I closed my eyes. I swallowed.

Johanna drew back, put her hand to her mouth.

I pointed to the picture, astounding even myself by my ability to ask Beryl in a very calm voice, "Where did you get that picture? Do you know those people? Are they related to you?" Could this little owl-like woman with the oversized glasses be a relative of mine? Some distant aunt? Did she know my aunt Rose?

She shook her head. "This is just a magazine picture, dear. I cut it out years ago. I've always thought the picture so lovely and romantic."

"*What* magazine?" I managed to ask.

"I have no idea. It was one of those magazines that had romance stories. Not many of them do anymore, you know. There was a time when every women's magazine had a romance story. I miss that."

Several women nodded in agreement. Several more looked up at me, concern across their faces.

"But *what* magazine? *When?*"

"Oh, my dear, that would be years ago now."

I kept looking at her and asked, "Did

you . . . Have you lived here a long time?"

She shook her head and said, "We moved here when Bert retired. That would be ten years."

"Then do you know these people?" I pointed at the picture.

Her eyebrows screwed together into one long brow across her face. I was conscious of time standing still, of the rest of the class regarding me, but I had to know.

"No, dear," she said. "I told you. This is just a picture from a magazine."

"But, um . . ." I couldn't take my eyes from the picture, the two of them, my parents in a stranger's hands.

I had lived with the story of my parents for as long as I could remember. They'd died in a car accident, the details of which were too painful for my aunt to ever fully talk to me about. Even when she was dying, she'd refused to tell me about the particulars of the accident. Was it a head-on collision? Was it a drunk driver? Had the car skidded out of control on icy or wet roads? When I would ask these questions, my aunt would simply turn her head away from me, tears at the edges of her eyes. I finally figured out that losing her sister was so painful to her that she couldn't, wouldn't talk about it. But I never stopped asking.

I looked around me. "Do any of you remember Allen and Sandra Simson? They would have lived here a long time ago, around thirty years now."

The ladies looked at each other and shook their heads.

I took a deep breath. "How about Rose Carlson? Do any of you know Rose Carlson? Or her sister, Sandra Carlson? That would have been her name before she was married."

All around were mystified head shakes. By now I felt so nauseated I could barely stand. I felt hot and cold all at once. Without further explanation, I fled to my little bathroom in the back, where I leaned both hands on the edge of the sink and looked at myself in the mirror. I was freezing. I was sweating. Peas of moisture beaded on my forehead, yet my throat was dry. I swallowed several times and just managed not to throw up. Breathe. Breathe, I told myself. Something else was bothering me, something I'd shoved to the back of my mind for all these years, something I didn't confront, couldn't. But something that was even now staring me in the face. I looked up at the reflection of my own face in the mirror above the sink. That beautiful, barefoot woman with the long hair was not my mother. The two in the picture were not my parents.

I could hear Johanna in the other room. "Well, ladies, let me go see how Marylee is. Keep leafing through the magazines and we'll be right back."

A moment later her hand was on my neck.

"Did you see the picture?" I asked.

"I did, Marylee. I did. But there's going to be a simple explanation. After the class, I'll come up to your apartment and we'll figure it all out." Her voice was soothing, and I was so glad she was my friend and that she was with me tonight.

"But why?" I asked. "Where did Beryl's picture come from? Where did my picture come from?"

After my aunt Rose had died and my engagement had fallen apart, I'd come here to Burlington, Vermont. It was the only thing I could really do. Even despite her Cassandra-like warnings, I was born here and had lived here for the three years prior to my aunt driving us out west. The secrets lay somewhere here in Burlington. I just had to find them. Of course, I had researched the accident. Through the years, I'd pawed through my aunt's things looking for pictures, looking for news articles, looking for death certificates. I'd found nothing. I'd searched my parents' names on the Internet, plus any reference to a car accident in Vermont many times, and had come up empty.

Someday I would stand at the graves of my parents. Someday I would find the rest of my family. For I knew there had to be more than just me and Aunt Rose.

Yet in the seven months I'd been here, I hadn't been able to find anyone who knew my parents or my aunt. I had scoured the cemeteries. No luck. None of the seniors in my afternoon scrapbooking class remembered the names Allen and Sandra Simson. I'd also worked my way through the newspaper archives at the public library so many times that the reference librarian was getting sick of seeing me come in. Yet I had found zilch. Google searches continued to yield nothing.

And now this! My first real clue in seven months and you'd think I'd be cheering and jumping up and down, yet here I was, my hand to my mouth to keep from throwing up.

Maybe there was a part of me that was afraid of what I would find. Or what I wouldn't find. Maybe, after all, there was nothing to find.

Two

After the last satisfied customer had left, I armed my store's security system and we went upstairs to my apartment, where Johanna brewed a big pot of chamomile tea.

Somewhere during the course of the evening it had started to rain. An appropriately cold rain which matched my mood slashed at the windows like knives.

I'd managed to muddle through the class with Johanna helping. I also apologized for running off like that, but offered no explanation. No one pressed for a reason. Johanna helped me lay out their initial efforts on tables in my back room. Everyone chatted while they gathered up their coats and purses. Next week at this same time they would be back to work on them. The class was a success. Everyone was happy. I was a mess.

The framed photo that I had talked to all these years was between us on the kitchen table. Johanna carefully removed the photo from the frame. "There might be something here," she said. "Maybe on the back."

"There's nothing," I told her. "Nothing on the back. Nowhere." And I should know. I'd scrutinized this picture many, many times for clues, a name of a photographer.

She said, "Why don't you get all the pictures of your parents together and then you can show them to all the people who come into the shop. You could even tack them up on some of the bulletin boards around town. There are so many things you could be doing, Marylee, if you want to find out who you're related to out here."

"*All* the pictures? This is the only picture I have." I was aware then that she was my friend, yet I had shared with her only carefully selected pieces of my life.

Her eyes went wide. "Really? Well, then, this one then, you show everyone this picture. You make copies. I could help you. We could put it in the paper, even."

"I can't. I can't explain it, I just can't do that." I didn't know if I could explain it properly to my friend, this reticence I felt. I didn't know if I could explain it properly to myself. It was all bound up in my aunt and her fears. When I was little, she hadn't even wanted me showing the picture to my friends. When I would ask her why not, her standard response would be, "You don't know who's out there."

I took a sip of my tea. My fingers were shaking so badly, I put the teacup down and stared into its depths. Johanna touched my hand. "How did your parents die?"

I sighed. "I don't know."

"You don't know?"

"I don't have all the information. My aunt wouldn't tell me. That's why I'm here. It's a long story."

"We have a whole pot of tea, and more where that came from."

So I told her. I told her I was born here in Burlington and after my parents died, my aunt Rose packed me up in her car and we drove clear across the country until we ended up in Portland, Oregon.

"Aunt Rose was the only mother I ever knew. She's been gone about a year." I bit my lip. "Ovarian cancer. I still miss her."

"Oh, Marylee."

I swallowed and continued. "But she kept warning me about Burlington. She told me not to come back here."

Johanna's eyes were wide. "And she never told you why?"

I took a swallow of tea and shook my head. "She was thrilled when I began going out with he-who-shall-not-be-named. I think she thought that was a surefire way to keep me from ever coming here to Burlington . . ."

I let my voice drift off and thought about that whole chapter of my life.

"He had stood with me throughout her six-month battle with cancer, he'd been the comfort I needed, my rock. The day after my aunt's funeral, he proposed." I said it quietly. "We ended up setting a date a year in the future. I lived that year in a kind of stupor, grieving for my aunt, my best friend and only living relative. I couldn't seem to focus on wedding plans. I couldn't seem to focus on anything.

"Three weeks before the wedding he bailed. I supposed it was only to be expected."

"Oh, Marylee!" Johanna came over and hugged me.

I blinked rapidly to keep the tears at bay. A shiver danced across my skin and I wrapped my arms around myself. It didn't help. I got up and turned up the thermostat. I glanced out the back window as I did so, and a truck rumbled down the back alley between the buildings on this rainy night.

Johanna took off her sweater. She was now down to a tank top in my warm kitchen, but bless her, she didn't say anything about the place being too hot. Yet, I could not rid myself of the chill. I wondered if I would ever be warm again, whole again, like a real person.

I continued. "Since I've come here, I try to think back. I try to remember this place, but I can't. I was too young. The first memory I have is of Aunt Rose driving. It was raining. I remember the sound of the windshield wipers, back and forth. For hours I watched them while my aunt kept driving and driving, not saying anything."

Johanna pulled her legs up underneath her and was sitting yogi-style on my kitchen chair. She was listening intently.

"When I was growing up my aunt was always so jumpy, so jittery. Any time there was a phone call that hung up she'd go crazy, running around locking all the doors and windows. I think we were the first house in the entire country to get a home security system. She was so nervous, my aunt was."

"Maybe she had a reason to be," Johanna said.

That statement clouded the air like smoke. I thought of the shadow that had moved across the coffee shop window tonight. Had I seen something? Or had it been a product of my overactive imagination? Was I becoming like my aunt Rose after all?

Johanna got up and tucked a quilt around my shoulders. She asked, "Have you been back to the house you lived in when you were here?"

"I don't even know where it is." I paused and looked at the droplets of rain clinging to my balcony window. "When I was about fourteen I went through a sort of rebellious period. I sneaked into my aunt's desk. She always kept it locked, but I knew where the key was. I was looking for something, anything, a picture, an address, a news clipping about the accident. But I found nothing. I had all her papers all over the bed, and that's when my aunt came through the door.

"I looked up expecting her to be furious. But she came and sat beside me and held me in her arms for a long time. She just held me and held me. And when I looked up I saw that she was crying, too. I think that was the beginning of us being close."

"You must miss her very much," Johanna said.

"We sat there for a while and then she said, 'I'm only trying to keep you safe. I've devoted my life to keeping you safe.' And then she said, 'Let's go make paper instead.' That was her answer to everything: Let's make paper."

"Paper?" Johanna looked at me, nearly spilling her tea.

I smiled, just a little. My aunt used to make paper. She had a special blender set aside just for her papermaking. We used to tear up old pieces of paper and then they would go in this blender with water. We had huge sinks in our basement and screens where we would lay out our pulp until it dried. She sold it by the sheet at markets and craft fairs. I told Johanna this, how my aunt was always saving bits and pieces of paper. She was into recycling before any-body else in the world was. "We would save old magazines and cut pictures out of them." I stopped, a strange idea niggling its way into my thinking. Had she somehow found that magazine in the trash, somehow took a picture of it, had it developed and then told me it was my parents? Is that how she had done it? But why? And if these two aren't my parents, then who are they and do they have any connection with me?

I picked up the photo and looked down at it. I had to admit that part of the attraction of this photo was the happiness this couple seemed to possess, the two of them, the way my mother looked into my father's eyes, the way he gazed down at her. Was this kind of love even possible? When I was a little girl I would make up elaborate scenarios about my parents. I put the photo facedown on the table.

Johanna picked up the photo, seemed to consider it, then said, "The place to begin with all of this is Evan, of course."

Despite myself I smiled. "We begin with *Evan?*"

"He's a photographer, Marylee. You know that." She leaned back and picked up her mug.

"A photographer's not going to know."

She leaned forward. "Sometimes he works with the police on forensics. Sometimes they get him to help them."

I hated to tell Johanna, but going to see Evan was not in the plans. He'd taken my friend out twice and dropped her. Plus, Evan had been engaged before. Whenever I thought about Evan, I couldn't help but think of Mark, my own ex-fiancé who'd dumped me when the going got too rough for him.

"He used to be an accountant," Johanna said. "Did you know that? He dropped that to pursue his art, his photography."

To me that was another strike against him; he can't commit to a woman and can't commit to a career. No, my friend could do a whole lot better than Evan Baxter.

"You should go see him."

I told her no, emphatically no.

THREE

I had the mirrors dream again that night. I've dreamed the mirrors dream, or a variation thereof for as long as I can remember. Sometimes I'm in a fun house and strange mirror faces taunt me. Sometimes I see mirror after mirror, the same reflection of myself going on and on forever and ever into infinity. Sometimes there are broken pieces of mirror and every time I pick them up I cut my fingers and they bleed. Sometimes I stand in front of a mirror and instead of seeing my reflection I see nothing. When I was little, I used to awaken screaming until Aunt Rose came in and prayed with me.

In tonight's dream, I was walking down a narrow hallway holding a piece of broken mirror. It belonged to one of the ladies in my evening class and I needed to catch up with her, tell her I had it. The edge of it had cut my hand and the blood left a trail behind me. I didn't care. I needed to find her. In my haste, I walked into a mirror. I turned to go back and was met with another mirror. I was lost and frantic as I tried to find my way out of the maze of my own reflections going in all directions.

I woke up, hot and miserable in the middle of the night. I'd left my heat up and the place was as close as a sauna. I turned down the thermostat. Outside it was still raining and I stood by the front window for a while.

I live on Main Street in Burlington, a busy street of shops and old New England–style three- and four-story houses. Across the street from me is a mystery bookshop in the lower level of a four-story dwelling that once was someone's grand residence, but was chopped into apartments and shops. Next to that is a consignment shop that features children's clothing. Right beside me is a coffee shop, and on the other side is a high-end bicycle and ski shop, this area of the country being known for two things, teddy bears and snow.

I focused on the bookstore and the huge cat that always sits in the window. He was there now, a dark mound on the window seat. The cat stretched and I watched its shadow move across the glass. I looked at it. Had it been the cat I'd seen earlier? I sighed and was about to get back to my bedroom when a movement on the street below caught my attention. I went to my bedroom and retrieved my glasses from my nightstand. There was a bobbing pinpoint of orange down below. It took me a moment to realize that this was the end of a cigarette. And the cigarette was attached to a person who was leaning against the back of a bus shelter. I watched him for a few moments, wondering that someone would be outside in the rain in the middle of the night. It took me several minutes to realize that this person was looking up at me. I stood very still, then backed away from the window. I felt rattled, unsettled. Before I went back to bed, I went to the door and made sure it was locked, the security system fully armed. Once the latch was pulled across the French doors I'd be secure. And then, feeling much like my aunt, I made a cup of chamomile tea — her favorite — and drank it in the kitchen.

The photo was still on my kitchen table, propped against the sugar bowl. I thought about what Johanna had said. See Evan? I sighed and looked down at the woman's face, that hint of a smile not for the photographer, but for the man — my father? —

who I've always thought was just about the handsomest man I'd ever seen.

I slept again after that, and dreamed that Aunt Rose was my real mother and that I had no father, and she'd forged my birth certificate and made up the story about my parents being in an accident just because she didn't want anyone to know that I was illegitimate. I got up, peeked around the side of the blind in the half light of early morning, but the cigarette smoker had gone. So had the cat.

Still tired, I went back to bed but tossed and turned until close to dawn, and when I finally did wake up, I had overslept. Since I'd forgotten to set the alarm, I ended up racing to get ready. I couldn't get my contacts in, so had to opt for a pair of thick glasses with black frames. I had purchased them a few years ago when I'd been in an artsy period, but now in the mirror all I saw were glasses. But my eyes were puffy from lack of sleep and there wasn't a whole lot I could do about it.

By the time I ran to the café for my coffee, my winking coffee stranger had already been and gone. I had no idea where he worked. I assumed it was somewhere around here, maybe even the mystery bookshop, although I'd never seen him in there when

I'd gone in for some reading material.

Where he came from and where he went each morning were a mystery. The only thing I knew about him was that he came in each morning at the same time for a dark roast coffee, which he took black. And, that he winked at me.

I was too late today, but with the way I looked this morning, it was just as well.

It was strange how I missed him, how disappointed I felt. If I believed in omens — which I didn't — I would have thought that not seeing him meant that this already bad day was going to get a whole lot worse. I walked into my shop, and today for the first time it seemed a desolate place. The rows upon rows of needlecraft kits and yarn and scrapbook supplies and watercolor kits and mirror pieces and mosaic tiles just looked like organized rows of so much junk. I went to the back and looked at Beryl's mirror tiles picture again. My parents. Or maybe not. But if they weren't my parents, who were they and how were they connected to me? If they were?

Before she left last night I told Johanna not to tell anyone about this picture. I knew she would respect my wishes. I didn't need to share the patheticness of my life with anyone else. Johanna had also carefully placed the photo between two sheets of cardboard and put it in a large envelope, still convinced that I would see Evan. I laid that next to my coat. When Barbara came in after lunch, I'd head over to the photography studio and force myself to deal with the infamous Evan Baxter.

I met the morning customers with cheery hellos. I helped two older women from my seniors' class pick out ribbons for their scrapbooks. I helped a young pregnant woman with yarn and doll faces. She kept going on about her new baby and decorating the room, and that made me feel blue. If my ex-fiancé hadn't jumped ship I would be married now. Quite possibly I'd even be pregnant. We'd talked about that. We'd wanted children right away. Mark, my ex-fiancé, worked as a computer programmer for a cable company. Everyone in church loved him where he was one of the leaders. He just couldn't stick it out with me when the going got tough. I sold the young mother-to-be some yellow yarn, a doll form and a pattern, and wished the new family well with a cheerful smile.

A gentlemanly old man named Marty Smythe and his friend Dot, both from my seniors' scrapbooking class came in and bought two children's needlepoint sets for

Dot's grandchildren. When I first met Marty and Dot, I figured them for an old married couple. Then one afternoon in the shop when Dot was talking to Barbara about ribbons, Marty whispered to me that he was going to ask Dot to marry him, he was just waiting for the right moment. I thought it was sweet. Barbara told me later that both Marty and Dot had lost their spouses a long time ago.

He looked at me and his eyebrows came together. "You okay?"

I nodded. "I must look horrible. I think I'm coming down with something." Coming down with something. Right, like a miserable life.

"Well, you take care, sweets," he said as I rang up the order.

I promised him I would and I watched him leave, the back of him, white hair bunching out under his black woolen cap. Something about the back of his hair under his cap made me start for a moment. I looked, but couldn't put a finger on it. I shook my head and went back to work.

Just after noon, Barbara came in cheerful and breezy the way she always does.

"How was the class?" she asked, unzipping her raincoat and hanging it in the back. "Oh, I can see how the class was. How lovely!" Barbara's one of those wonderfully warm maternal types who talk nonstop. I knew she'd have lots of good advice for me if I told her about my parents and the picture questions. But I didn't. I couldn't. Not yet. She stopped her chattering and looked at me. "Are you okay, Marylee?"

I attempted a laugh. "Everyone keeps asking me that. I think it's my glasses. I don't usually wear them, so when I do, everyone looks at me strangely."

"I think they're very charming. They make you look quite studious."

I told her that I hadn't slept well, and that when I'd gotten up in the night someone had been standing down across the street smoking in the bus shelter. "It unnerved me," I said. "I didn't sleep much after that."

"Well I don't blame you!" Her eyes were wide. "Did you call the police?"

"Last I heard it wasn't a crime to stand in a bus shelter and smoke in the middle of the night."

"Still, it would be kind of spooky, I'd say, someone looking up at your window like that."

I looked down at my hands. "It was just somebody smoking." But it wasn't, was it? I had seen a face upturned in my direction.

A little while later, I told her I had an errand to run and left her in charge of the store. I walked the three blocks through a gray drizzle to Evan Baxter Photography. I wasn't sure this was the wisest thing I'd ever done. After what he had done to Johanna, not to mention to his fiancée, I knew I should probably just steer clear of him.

I was surprised that his store was so close to my own. I had done a bit of walking in the neighborhood, but never in this direction. Usually when I head out I go down Main Street, and then turn right at the ferry terminal and into the waterfront park. Most of the time, when I get to the coast guard building, I turn around and go home.

Evan Baxter Photography is located in an upscale brick building just up from the railroad yard. In the same building is a design studio and a law office. Inside it was quiet and no one seemed to be around. There was a ring-for-service bell on the counter, but I hate those things, even though I have one myself. They sound so impatient and demanding to me. After standing at the counter for a few moments and having no one appear, however, I pressed it tentatively and looked around.

The photos on the wall were arranged as if in a gallery. There were insects on branches, close-ups of flowers and faces.

There were lots of faces; old people with expressive smiles, children on swings, wedding pictures, graduation pictures, photos of quilts that caught my attention for a while. I could name some of the patterns: log cabin, cross weave and tessellating flowers. Aunt Rose was also a master quilter and in my apartment I have a small quilting frame, a graduation gift from her. I'm attempting to finish the quilt she started before she got sick.

But the photo that drew me, the picture that caused me to stand there unmoving, was one of a small girl standing beside a campfire. She was young, maybe ten, and wore scuffy pink sneakers and a hooded zippered sweatshirt that was opened to reveal a pink T-shirt. She was pointing at the flames.

I marveled that Evan was able to capture the vivid hues of the fire and how they were reflected in the solemn face of the girl as she pointed.

Close behind, very close behind me was a sound.

"You didn't get your medium nonfat latte today." I jumped, turned and found myself face-to-face with my winking coffee stranger. I muffled a gasp, put a hand to my mouth.

"Sorry," he said. "I didn't mean to startle you."

"It's okay. I . . . uh . . ." I felt my face flush. "I didn't hear you. I was looking at the picture." I was conscious of the fact that I couldn't look any worse if I tried; glasses, flat hair tied back, red eyes and any makeup I did have on, being long ago smeared off by my sniffles. I hoped desperately that I didn't have mascara lines running down my cheeks. And then I wondered, what in the world was *he* doing here, anyway? Maybe he was here buying film on his lunch hour.

"Are you, uh, are you a photographer?" I asked him stupidly. I was backing away slightly, aware, so aware of him standing close to me. I caught a whiff of a kind of musky aftershave.

"Do you like that one?" He pointed at the picture of the girl.

I nodded. "It's very, um, vivid. The colors. The girl. She sort of, um, reminds me of myself when I was a girl. She looks so sad, somehow." My voice trailed off. Why for goodness' sake was I going on about this to a complete stranger? And why did I think he would care?

He said, "That one is sort of special to me."

It was special to him? How could it be

special to him? Someone had started a blender in my stomach.

"You asked if I was a photographer. I try to be," he said.

I nodded some more. I felt like a bobble-head doll. He was even better looking close-up than across the crowded coffee shop. And what was I thinking with these thoughts, anyway? I needed to find Evan Baxter and get out of here.

"Are you in the market for a camera? Digital, perhaps?" he asked.

I shook my head. "No, um . . ." I swallowed. "I'll just wait here for the owner. I need to speak to Evan Baxter about something."

He raised one eyebrow, and then did the wink thing again. "Well, you're looking at him."

It took me a moment to figure out what he said. "I'm looking at him?"

He nodded.

"You're Evan Baxter?"

"In the flesh." He was smiling broadly.

"You *can't* be!"

"Was last time I looked at my driver's license."

"But, but . . ." I sputtered. "I didn't know you were Evan Baxter." My hand flew to my mouth. "You really are Evan Baxter?"

He grinned. "I really am."

"Oh . . . Oh . . ."

"I'm glad you like the campfire photo," he said.

I kept sniffing and feeling foolish. I felt around in my pocket for a Kleenex, but of course I didn't have one when I needed one. I kept nodding. I still hadn't managed to say anything. I could almost hear what he was thinking: *Why won't this stupid, simpering woman get to the point?*

Time to do just that. I took a breath. "I came in because, well, I need some help identifying a photograph. I've been told you might be able to help me. I would pay you, of course. Whatever you think is fair." I tried to keep my voice businesslike. "I would like to know where a photo was taken, and who took it. This photo I have complemented a short story in a women's magazine."

"Let's see what you've got." He led me back to the counter where I opened up the manila envelope and took the photo out from between the two sheets of taped cardboard. He glanced at it. "You want to know who these people are?"

"No . . . I . . . I already know who they are." I put my hand to my mouth, forced myself to breathe, breathe, and get back to my all-business self. "Yes. Maybe I would like to know that. And I need to know, um, who took this picture and maybe what magazine it was in. This is the original. I want to know . . . I don't know." My voice broke. And at that point I realized that I really didn't know what I wanted to know at all. Why was I here? What I wanted to know was if anyone in this entire city of Burlington could tell me about my parents, but I couldn't tell him that. He was a stranger.

He picked up the photo and studied it, and his eyes lingered there a bit too long. I swear I could hear him softly gasp. Then just as quickly, he recovered. When he brushed his curly hair out of his eyes, I wondered if I'd only imagined that flinch.

He bent his head so all of his hair fell forward into his eyes. As he spread out the edges of the photo with his fingers, I unwillingly found myself looking at his hands. I always think hands tell a lot about a man. His were strong and articulate. I could imagine him fiddling with camera settings, adjusting a shot until he got it just right, not being happy until it was.

Stop that, Marylee, I told myself. This guy dropped Johanna without so much as a how do you do. He's someone you definitely want to steer clear of. So, why was I here, trusting him with one of the most important things in my life?

From underneath the counter he got a magnifying glass.

"This picture looks old," he said. "The styles. These two look like hippies. It's artistically done, though. Nice. Romantic." And he looked at me and winked.

"I think it's around thirty years old." I kept my demeanor as businesslike as I could. "I understand you do forensic work for the police department."

He shifted his position. "Sometimes." He put the photo down and looked at me. "Okay, here's what we can do. We can compare it to data banks of stock photos," he said. "Although if it was in a magazine thirty years ago that might pose a challenge."

"You said 'we'?"

"My assistant, Mose, is a whiz at dating old photos. He might be able to help. I'm sure he'll have some ideas, in any case."

"I would also like information about certain parts of the photo." I pointed out some duskiness along one side. "I'd always assumed these shadow things to be trees or some sort of bushes or building, but I don't know."

"It's quite faint," he said. "It could be just

something in the photo itself, or on the paper."

I nodded.

"We could digitize this, maybe enlarge these shadows, see what we can come up with."

"By all means." I handed him one of my Crafts and More business cards. "I'm Marylee Simson." I tried to sound as professional as possible despite my bleary eyes, bad hair and shaking knees.

"I already know your name." And he winked at me. "And I already know your shop. It's nice to finally meet you officially."

And all the way back to Crafts and More all I thought about was *I can't believe it. I cannot believe it! What am I going to tell Johanna? What on earth am I going to tell Johanna?*

That afternoon Johanna called me at the shop between her classes, as I knew she would. I was dreading this. How to tell her? What to say?

"So?" she said.

"So?" I answered.

"So, did you take the picture to Evan?"

"I took the picture to Evan."

"And?"

"And what?"

"And *what?* Isn't he absolutely irresistible?"

"He's . . ." This was going to be harder than I thought. "He's, uh, he's got the photo. He's looking at it . . ."

"Well, duh, I figured that much," she said.

I heard the bells chime at my door signifying a customer. "I gotta go. A customer arriveth!"

"You will come to my house tonight and tell me everything that happened."

It was an order, and I couldn't help but chuckle. "Okay," I said. "I'll bring my homemade pizza."

When I hung up the phone I saw that I'd left my apartment key in the door. I pulled it out and pocketed it before heading back out to the store.

There is a back door to this place with stairs leading up to my apartment. I keep that door locked during the day. When you come in either the front door to the shop or the back door, you first have to unlock it with a key, and all the keys are different. Then you have to punch in the six-digit security code. When you get up the stairs to my apartment, there's another lock, another key and another security-code pad.

All thanks to my paranoid aunt.

For the rest of the afternoon I chided

myself. What kind of a friend keeps something like this from a best friend? I should have blurted it right out. *Your Evan is the one who winks at me every morning! That's the kind of guy he is. He breaks off an engagement and then goes out and drops someone after two dates with no explanation and then winks at someone else. What is he doing, just going down the line of available females?* I'd tell her all of this tonight. I started practicing ways to tell her.

We close at five on Wednesdays, so I had ample time to do up my special pizza from scratch. I'd make enough dough for two pizzas and put one in the freezer. As I was working on measuring the yeast and kneading the dough, it felt to me as if I were making a peace offering, something to make Johanna feel better when I broke the news. I'd add sliced tomatoes to the top because I know she likes fresh sliced tomatoes on her pizza.

I was just setting the dough to rise for a few minutes when I looked over at my balcony door and noticed something odd. The pull-across latch was pushed back. Had I unlocked this door? I couldn't remember. It seemed unlikely, though. I stepped back, stared at it, thought of my key left in my door. Two key-related oddities in one day; I *was* turning into my aunt.

I opened the French doors and stepped onto my balcony and looked over the railing. My aunt would approve of this balcony. There was no way anyone could climb up here. No fire escape led to it. There weren't even any balconies close by where you could jump across, if a person was so inclined. Theoretically, I should be able to leave it unlocked and be fine. You'd have to be Spider-Man to get up here. My wicker rocker was undisturbed. I sat in it for a few minutes before the chill evening air drove me back inside to where my crust was happily rising.

At seven sharp I was standing on the doorstep of Johanna's cute house. She lives just north of the city on a little island on Malletts Bay. It's only a few minutes from the downtown core where I live, but driving up Coates Island Road is like driving into another country. I drove past the marina on Malletts Bay, with its huge yachts, many of which were already shrink-wrapped in white. Soon, I was told, Lake Champlain would freeze so solid you could drive a truck across it.

Coates Island, where Johanna lives, is a private island of mostly summer cottages. Johanna lives here year-round in the last house, she says, before they quit plowing the road. It's a place she could never afford on her professor's salary, but it's been in her family for many generations. The only downside is that her big family of brothers and sisters and uncles and aunts descends on her all summer long.

Johanna's place is just like her — funky and cottagey and filled with mismatched dishes and chairs, all bought at garage sales. But instead of looking tacky, it looks as if each piece has been carefully chosen from high-end antique stores. She has this way of assembling a bunch of disparate pieces into a charming whole, and that includes the clothes she wears.

As soon as I entered her house, she came right over and hugged me.

"Evan," she said. "You have to tell me about Evan! You have to tell me *everything!*" She looked so cute this evening. Her thick hair was caught up in a scrunchie on the top of her head, like a cockeyed waterspout.

I dropped my jacket on the back of a wooden kitchen chair. "You could do a whole lot better than Evan Baxter," I told her.

She stopped a moment in her table setting and raised her eyebrows. "What? What happened? What do you mean by that?"

"I just think you could do better than Evan Baxter. That's all." I was careful not to meet her eyes.

"Marylee, tell me what happened. Don't leave anything out. Wasn't he able to help you with your picture?"

"I need to talk to you about Evan." I placed my pizza on the table. "This is really important. Evan? He's the guy who winks at me in the coffee shop every morning. The very one."

If I could have chosen all of the reactions on her part, I never would have chosen the one that she exhibited. Instead of looking horrified, her eyes opened wider and she leaned back against her counter and laughed. It was a gleeful, spontaneous laugh.

"Johanna?" I squinted at her over my glasses.

"Oh, Marylee!" She leaned forward and put her hand on my shoulder. "This is so funny, so totally funny. What a strange coincidence."

"Well, yeah."

"Now you know how cute he is."

"Johanna, you're not getting it. He's irresponsible. He takes you out. Doesn't call back. Winks at me, a total stranger."

Her back was to me as she poured two Diet Cokes. "Let's have the pizza," she said.

She was hurt, I could tell. The laughter was just a cover-up, but I didn't know what to do or say. Perhaps I shouldn't have told her. But, of course I had to. Friends don't keep stuff like this from their friends. We took our slices and Cokes into her front room overlooking the water.

She took a bite of the pizza, proclaimed it wonderful and then said, "Did you hear that Barbara's son Jared is home from Guatemala?"

I knew she was changing the subject on purpose, but I had no desire to bring the subject back to Evan, so I said, "That's all I've been hearing about."

I took a long drink of Coke. Through the trees, the gray water of Malletts Bay looked as solid as iron.

Barbara's eldest son had taken a six-month leave of absence from his police job to work on a mission project in Guatemala. Barbara and her husband, Harold, had invited some of the people his age from church to a supper where he'd be talking about the trip and showing pictures.

"I know Jared," Johanna said. "You haven't met him, but you'd like him. He'd be perfect for you."

Clever ploy, I thought. Get me interested in Jared so she wouldn't have to worry about Evan and me. I leaned forward and touched my friend's arm. "Johanna, you don't have to worry. I am not interested in Evan." I'm not interested in that type of guy anymore — all charm and no substance, I wanted to add, but didn't. "And I'm not interested in Jared either. I've had enough of men for a while. All men."

Four

For the next two days I studiously avoided Evan. I went for my coffee a whole hour earlier. I knew this wouldn't last. He had my photo and would be calling. But maybe the few days would give me time to organize my thoughts, and maybe my emotions. My problem was I'd let a morning wink take over my life. I seriously wanted to believe what I had told Johanna last night, that Evan held no attraction for me whatsoever, that no man did. But, unfortunately, I found myself thinking about him more, not less.

On the second day of not seeing Evan, Marty and Dot came in to buy a paint-by-numbers set. "It's for Dot's granddaughter," Marty said. "It's her birthday tomorrow."

"How nice," I said.

"There's going to be a big party," Dot added.

"Have a wonderful time." I put their purchase in a bag and looked at Marty. The other day something about him had seemed strangely familiar. Today that feeling was gone. Today he was just an ordinary nice-looking older gentleman, obviously in love with his lady friend.

On the third day, Evan Baxter came into my shop. I was in the back unpacking boxes of yarn when I recognized his voice.

"Is the lady of the shop in?"

I held my breath.

"Just a minute," Barbara said. "And you are?"

"Evan. Evan Baxter."

"Oh yes, of course!" she exclaimed. "My husband, Harold, bought a camera from you some time ago, and talked about your lovely photographs."

"I remember him."

"Marylee," she singsonged. "Someone here to see you."

I wiped my hands on my Crafts and More apron and went out to the front. As soon as I got there I wished I'd had time to run a brush through my hair. Still, today it didn't quite look as bad as it had three days ago. At least I'd been up early enough this morning to blow-dry some life into it.

"Hey," he said. Then he winked at me.

"Hello," I said.

"I've missed you in the mornings."

"I've been busy."

"Too busy for a nonfat latte?"

"I've been getting to the shop earlier." I ran my hands up and down my apron. All of the sentences I'd rehearsed for this occasion had flown completely out of my head. Plus, Barbara was observing this whole conversation with amusement. Since she'd come to work for me, she'd been like a mother hen, trying to hook me up with every available guy she knew, especially with Jared. I hadn't quite confided in her that since I'd been trampled on and tramped over by Mark, I was interested in no one. Not even her eldest son Jared.

"So, did you find anything about the picture?" I asked him.

He nodded. "You have time for coffee?"

"Right now?" I glanced at my watch. "I'm working now. There's a lot to do." I looked around me. The shop was dead. We hadn't had a customer in half an hour and new boxes of fabric supplies were mostly unpacked.

"You go," Mother Barbara said, shooing me out. "Have a coffee." Then to Evan she said, "This young woman is working way too hard. And not sleeping. Plus, there are men outside her door."

"Barbara!" I shrieked at her.

"No, what I mean is, she sees people smoking down in the street in the middle of the night, so she can't sleep at night. That would be enough to put anyone off their Wheaties."

Why, I wondered, had I shared that little tidbit of my life with her?

Evan raised an eyebrow and a worried look crept across his face. "People? Outside your house?"

"It's nothing," I said. "It was one night. A few nights ago when it was raining. Someone was in the bus shelter across the street smoking."

"You said *he?* It was a man?" he said, looking worried.

"I don't know. I couldn't tell. But it was nothing. It was someone stepping outside for a smoke in the middle of the night. What's so odd about that? Most people don't smoke in their houses anymore, so what do you do when you want a smoke in the middle of the night? That's all it was. I don't even know why I brought it up."

At the time I'd been so sure the person, either man or woman, had been looking up at my apartment, at me, even. But the more I thought about it, the more fanciful that idea became. I needed to steel myself against becoming like my aunt.

Evan and I went next door to the coffee shop. He ordered a house dark roast black and without even asking got me a nonfat latte. He also brought a huge, drippy cinnamon bun to our table with two forks. The two-forks bit seemed a little too chummy to me.

He paid for the coffees, which made me feel somewhat uncomfortable. I had hired him, so I should be paying, right? What does one do in these situations?

"Your sales clerk is an interesting woman," he told me.

"She's great. Although she says exactly what's on her mind. Very blunt, as you may have noticed."

"That's refreshing, though. You've got a nice shop there. You've fixed it up well."

"Thank you," I said. I looked at his hands again as they deftly cut the cinnamon bun in two with a plastic knife.

"I was halfway interested in it when it went up for sale," he said. "I pay rent in the spot I'm in now. It would be nice to own something outright."

"It wasn't cheap."

"I know. That's why I stayed where I am." He grinned and I wondered what I was doing here making small talk with Johanna's soul mate. I had a niggling fear that Johanna would walk in and see us like this. The thought made me uneasy.

He asked me where I was from and all I said was *out west.* He drank his coffee and said he'd grown up here in Burlington. I thought about the little note of surprise in his eyes when he'd seen the picture for the first time. Even though there was a part of me that still wondered if the picture was my parents, I needed a starting point. Were the couple in the picture connected to me? And why had my aunt lied to me — if she had?

I looked across at Evan and tried to guess his age. He couldn't be much older than me. Would he remember the accident that supposedly took my parents' lives? Should I ask him? I shook off that thought. I was beginning to realize just how big the city of Burlington was. I had no idea if I was even looking in the right section of town. Maybe I needed to be in Colchester, or Winooski, or Essex Junction.

He took off his glasses and cleaned them with an edge of the paper napkin. I watched him do that, wondering why his every little motion held such interest for me. I asked, "You said you have information about the picture?"

"I do."

I waited while he put his glasses back on

and placed the manila envelope with the photograph on the table. I reached for it at the same time he did and our hands touched. I pulled mine away quickly. For an awkward moment, neither of us said anything. I cleared my throat, and finally said, "So what did you find out?"

"I'm pretty sure it's a composite."

"Come again?"

"A composite. I'm thinking that the two people may have been superimposed on the backdrop of the lake. That was how they manipulated photos twenty-five years ago. Now, we have computer programs which do the same thing."

"So, this might not be Lake Champlain? It might not be here at all?"

"It might not be."

"How do you know that?"

He pointed. "I've enlarged this part of it. Do you see this bush in the foreground? Do you see the shadow it casts? It's very subtle."

I looked. "A bit," I said. "Maybe."

"Have a look at the couple. They cast no shadow. A computer-generated photo manipulation would have taken care of that. Or a good photo manipulator could manually add a very faint shadow here." He pointed.

"But . . . But it looks okay to me. I mean

they could be there, couldn't they? By Lake Champlain?"

He put one finger in the air. "There's more. Look at their bare feet. If they were standing on the stones like that, the feet of the man, of the woman, too, for that matter, would be making more of an impression on the ground beneath them. Plus, I can't see people standing on stones with bare feet anyway. Can you?"

"But people could, couldn't they?"

"Maybe," he said.

"So, this is a fake?"

"Oh no, it's not a fake. It's a real photograph. It's not some sort of a painting or reproduction, if that's what you mean."

That's not what I meant, but I didn't tell him what I meant because I wasn't sure myself.

"What about these shadows along the side?" I asked.

"To me they look like some sort of building. I couldn't figure it out, but Mose is still working on that."

I took a drink of my latte. "I have to ask you something. When you first looked at this picture it was like you'd seen it before. Had you?"

He looked down at his coffee and shook his head.

"Then why did you flinch when you looked at it? I know I saw you do that."

He looked at me. I hadn't noticed before how blue his eyes were. "I didn't flinch. I thought it was familiar when I first looked at it, but then I realized I was mistaken."

"Familiar, how?" I asked.

He shrugged. "I'm not sure."

"Were the people familiar? Did you think you recognized them?" My hands were clasped so tightly around my paper coffee cup that I was in danger of squishing the cup and spilling coffee all over us. I let up on my grip and repeated my question. "Do you know these people?"

He looked me square in the eyes. "No, Marylee. I don't know who they are."

I repeated my question. "Then why did you flinch?"

He shrugged and said, "I don't know."

I looked away from him. Unbidden tears threatened at the edges of my eyes. Finally, I turned back and said, "You mentioned stock photos the last time we talked."

"Mose hasn't found anything yet."

I nodded.

"This photo must mean a lot to you."

I didn't answer him. Instead I took a sip of my coffee. "This photo is connected to Burlington and to me. And I need to find out what the connection is between these people and me."

"I'll continue to look into it. It'll be my number-one priority." His voice was gentle when he told me this.

"I would like that. Thank you very much."

We drank our coffees in silence for the next few minutes. He cut another piece of cinnamon bun and said, "I was wondering about something else, Marylee. Would you ever consider going to dinner with me?"

I blinked. Had I heard him correctly?

"I . . ." I looked at my hands. "No. I don't know. I'm sorry. Things are sort of, well, complicated right now, Evan. I'm really sorry."

"That's okay."

"No, really, I'm sorry."

"Well then. Have the rest of the cinnamon bun."

Suddenly I wanted to be away from here. I made a point of looking at my watch. "I have to get back to my store," I said. "I'm so sorry."

"It's okay."

I got up, grabbed my picture and fled.

Back at the store, I realized I had my picture. I'd told him to keep working on the picture, and here I'd walked off with it. This meant I'd have to somehow come face-to-face with him again if I wanted him to continue looking into where it came from.

And then there was the little matter of paying him for his services. He'd done all this work for me. What should I do? Here I was a supposedly savvy businesswoman who'd managed to come up with enough money to purchase outright a prime piece of real estate, set up a business and do comparatively well, yet I was standing in the middle of my store feeling whimpery. And, if I admitted it to myself, just the teensiest bit afraid. I was getting closer to my parents and I was afraid, just a little, of what I might find when I got there.

"Hey, while you were gone, I . . ." Barbara began. At the same time the door jangled signifying an incoming customer and for one horrid moment I thought it was Evan. I clasped my hand to my mouth, but the thin little man who entered was nothing like Evan. Barbara recognized him from her knitting club and introduced us. They wandered over to the yarn supplies and I made my way to the back room, the picture of my parents in my hand. I shoved it inside the phone book. I took two deep breaths and came out into my store again.

While Barbara rang up yarn and needles

for her knitting compatriot, I waited on two customers, a mother and daughter who inquired about crocheting classes and ended up buying bits and pieces of ribbon and some paper and glue for a scrapbook they were making about their dog.

I waited on customers, straightened shelves and listened to Barbara talk about her sons, all the while looking at the door. Wondering if Evan would come back.

"Hey," I could hear him say. *"You left and took the picture."*

"I know, I know," I would say. *"I'm sorry about running off. Let me get the photo for you."* And I would, and then we'd end up going to dinner. And getting married and living happily ever after.

No. Not going to happen.

When I finally ascended the stairs to my apartment, my phone message light was blinking. Three messages. I pressed the button.

"Marylee? Evan here . . ." I sat down on my kitchen chair and caught my breath. "I'm sorry if something I said upset you when we were having coffee earlier. I certainly didn't mean to."

The second was also from him. "Sorry about the second phone call here, but if you still want me to help with the photo, I will.

I would be happy to even if we don't have dinner. If you want to come by with the photo again, I'll take another look at it."

The third message was from my security company. I called the number they left and through a series of voice-mail prompts, I ended up having to plug in my current security password code. I thought that was a bit odd, but complied. This was the second time they'd called wanting this information. I'd given it the first time. But I trusted them. They were a good security company and came highly recommended.

After I erased the messages, I decided I needed to talk with Johanna. She was my best friend and deserved to know that Evan had asked me to dinner. It was only fair, right? I called her, and breathed with relief when she didn't answer. I hung up without leaving a message.

Five

Something loud and irritating was blasting through my dreams. My alarm clock? I rubbed the sleep out of my eyes and glanced at the red lights of the digital readout beside me: 2:31 a.m. No, not my alarm clock, but someone's car methodically honking, the sound that happens if you suddenly press the honk button on your car's remote instead of Unlock Door. I knew that sound. I'd embarrassingly done exactly that in parking lots more times than I cared to admit. Whoever owned the car in the alley better hurry up and realize that their horn was honking and waking up every sleeping neighbor within a half-mile radius.

And then I sat upright and flicked on my bedside lamp as I came to realize that *my* car was the only car in the alley. Quickly I fumbled out of bed, entangling myself in the sheets, falling on the floor, then righting myself, locating the light switch and finding my way blearily into my kitchen and to my balcony doors. All the while the car was honking, honking, honking. Yes, my little Saturn was making all that racket.

I'd been told there are only three times when this happens: when you push the horn button, when someone is trying to get in your car, or when it's a defect in the car itself. My ex-fiancé had had a car that kept doing this in rainy weather, and it had ended up being due to moisture between the car door and the frame. But his was an old car and mine was brand-new! I scrambled around my apartment looking for my car keys.

I finally found them in a dish on my kitchen counter and grabbed them. Did this mean I was going to have to go down the back stairs and outside? I looked out at the rainy skies and groaned at the thought. I would try something else.

I opened the French doors, stepped out onto the cold balcony and, leaning over as far as I could, I aimed my remote at the car and pressed the horn button. Mercifully, it stopped. It was only when I got back into bed that the shivering wouldn't stop. A few moments later I got up and checked that the bolt was firmly across the French doors, even though I had just done this.

As I lay in bed, finally, with the light still on, I realized just how like my aunt I was becoming: single, alone, frightened. When I was a teenager I had vowed that I would never be like her. I remember coming upon her in the middle of the night drinking tea in the kitchen after a middle-of-the-night wrong number.

"Who could it be?" she'd asked. "Calling innocent people in the middle of the night. It has to be something, don't you think? Some prowler. I'm going to call the police."

I'd screamed at her, "It's just a stupid wrong number! Don't go postal!"

I slept fitfully for the rest of the night, waking every hour to glance at the digital readout: 3:32, 4:46, 6:02. Thankfully I didn't dream about the mirrors. I couldn't have. I didn't sleep long enough.

Evan was in the coffee shop when I got there the following morning. He winked but I left before he had a chance to come over and talk to me.

Midway through the afternoon, Barbara came out to where I was arranging scrap-book supplies on a top shelf. I thought she was going to remind me for the umpteenth time about the supper meeting at her house in two days with Jared in attendance, but she said, "A box came. It's not inventory.

It's personal from Portland. I opened it by mistake."

I hurried to the back. The shoe box was from my aunt's lawyer and contained a series of sealed envelopes. There was a letter on the top addressed to me:

> Dear Marylee Simson,
> We are moving from our office and I found this box amongst some papers. A long time ago your aunt, Rose Carlson, gave it to me for safekeeping. I have been remiss in not sending it to you sooner.
>
> Regards,
> R. E. Hoffman, Attorney at Law

The four envelopes were labeled: First 6 Months, Months 6–12, First House, and Other Misc. Underneath the envelopes was what looked like an old ledger book, faded and worn. I opened to the first page. It looked like a store accounts book, of the kind that I might keep for Crafts and More if everything wasn't all on computer now. I wiped some of the dried grunge from it with a paper towel. There was no name on the front, but I knew without even looking at it that it belonged to the craft store my aunt had worked at for all of my growing-up years. At some point it might be fun to compare prices and stock with my own store. I put it aside because I wanted to see what was in the envelopes. Eagerly I opened the First 6 Months one. It contained four photos. All were of my aunt and me when I was a small girl. In one of the pictures I was wearing a lavender coat, purple ribbons in my hair and black patent leather shoes, as if dressed for Sunday school. I remembered those shoes. I would have worn them all week if I could. Aunt Rose would make me change into sneakers for outdoor play while I fought and fought to wear what I called my "fancy shoes."

The second picture was of me on Santa's lap. I remembered how frightened I'd been of this big bearded man. The two others were of me and Aunt Rose beside a snowman. I quickly figured out that these photos were of the first six months we'd lived in Portland, Oregon.

Months 6–12 contained five pictures in total, again of Aunt Rose and me. I studied my aunt who was just about the same age as I am now. I saw the determined set of her jaw, and wondered what would prompt her to take her sister's child and drive clear across the country?

In one of the pictures, we were sitting together at a picnic table next to a tree in our backyard. I knew that when we'd first moved to Portland, we'd lived in an apartment for a time. My aunt had told me that. A year later we moved to the small square bungalow that I grew up in, the only place I really remember, the place I sold a year ago to come out here and buy this place.

I worked carefully through the contents of the box, envelope by envelope, looking always, always for pictures of my parents. But there were none of the beautiful couple, a couple so handsome that they were used as a magazine illustration for a romance story. But had I really expected some?

In the envelope marked Other Misc. were several pictures of people I didn't know. The only one I recognized was the owner of the craft shop where Rose had worked. She was a large woman and the only person I have ever known who wore knitted skirts. Rose and I used to laugh about that, her big skirts that looked like overgrown sweaters.

In that same envelope were a few photos of the craft shop where Aunt Rose had worked. I remembered that store, walking there after school and sitting at the high table in the room in the back and doing my homework or watching videos on the little TV there while my aunt finished up for the day.

The fact that there were photos in the box surprised me. My aunt was not one for pictures. She always said she looked terrible in pictures and refused to have any taken. "The camera isn't kind to me," she used to say. As a result, there were only scant photos in my childhood house. I put the snapshots back into their respective envelopes. Later, when I had more time I'd go through the store accounting book.

After Barbara left at five, I did some cleaning up and took the money out of the cash register and back to the safe where it would stay until I could get it to the bank in the morning. Out of my small fridge in the back, I grabbed a vanilla yogurt and plugged in the kettle. I would look at the pictures again. I spread them out on the table as if I were playing a giant game of solitaire. I could sit here and look at pictures of me and my aunt and watch the front at the same time. Closing was at five-thirty.

A few moments later I heard the entry bells jingle. I looked up to see a smiling Johanna. "Just thought I'd stop by," she said.

"Come on back," I said. "You want some instant soup? Or some tea? Kettle's on."

"Thanks."

"Your hair looks nice," I told her.

"You think so?" She fingered it. "My sister

did it for me. I can't do French braids on my own. She is a fashionista par excellence."

Her sister. I tried to hide my wistful expression. This happened all the time when people talked about their families.

"What are these?" Johanna asked, looking over my shoulder.

I told her.

"Wow!" she said, picking up a picture. "This is you? Oh, look at you, you used to be so cute."

"What do you mean, *used to be?*" I said, doing a little smile and striking a pose.

"And this is your aunt Rose?" she said, picking up another. She looked at it and at me. "I still think you look like her at that age. Sort of."

"That's what I'm told," I said. "I called you earlier."

"I know, I saw your caller ID on my phone. That's why I'm here." She found a semi-clean coffee mug beside my sink, rinsed it out and dumped in the contents of an instant soup packet from containers I keep above my sink.

I took a breath. "I wanted to talk to you about Evan."

She sat down and blinked at me. "What about him?"

"He asked me out to dinner, and I'm only

telling you this because it underscores my point of the type of guy he is. He breaks his engagement, switches career midstream, goes out with you twice, doesn't —"

"Three times."

"Pardon?"

"Three times. We went out three times. There was almost a fourth, but I wouldn't call it a date. We happened to run into each other at the park. Well, accidentally on purpose and so we ended up sitting on the bench talking. But I guess you couldn't call that a date because he didn't know ahead of time and we —"

"Johanna! You're not listening to me. He asked me out. On a date. Actually, he wanted to know if I would ever consider going to dinner with him."

Her eyes went wide. "Are you going?"

"Of course not!" But even as I said this I thought about that one little piece of his curly hair that fell onto his forehead.

She sighed, looked at me seriously and said, "Marylee, I need to tell you something. I thought about this all last night and the day before. I didn't even sleep last night, I thought about it so much. I even prayed about it." She sighed and then went on. "I just want you to know that if you do decide to go out with him it's okay with me. It really is. Maybe it's time for me to think about the fact that he's a lost cause." But even as she said this, I thought, I won't hurt her. No. Evan Baxter was a closed subject.

We ended up talking about Jared and how in a couple of days I'd get to meet him. Again, I felt as if Johanna was foisting him on me. Well, maybe I'd like him. Who knows? But I quickly quashed that thought. I had too much on my plate to be thinking about guys.

It was the night of my second mirror-arts class. Which meant it had been exactly one week since I'd talked to the picture of my parents. It had also been almost a week since I'd met Evan face-to-face.

My ladies were all there, including Johanna, and they worked hard placing the mirror pieces where they would best reflect and enhance the pictures they'd chosen. I told them about light and reflection, and even spent a few minutes talking about the history of mirrors.

Getting excited over art and design, I could almost forget Evan for the time being, and Jared, too. But not my mother or father. Every time I saw Beryl's picture I would think how I had told this photo all my dreams and hopes and plans. I've never kept a journal. Instead my journal was talking to this picture every day.

Partway through the evening, Felicia, the woman who sat next to Beryl, looked down at the magazine picture and said, "You asked us last week whether those people looked familiar to us. Well, I got to thinking. I have to say that woman, she *does* look familiar, don't you think? I just can't place where."

Another woman peered down at picture. "Not really. Maybe just a little."

"Who does she look like?" I asked.

A woman named Ann looked at me and then at the picture and said, "Well, I think she looks maybe a little like you, Marylee."

I gasped softly. "Me?"

"Don't you think?" And the others looked at the picture and then at me.

"Maybe a little," someone else said.

"Well," I said, trying to regain my composure, "if my hair was a yard long and blond, and if I was way slimmer and if my lips weren't so thin, maybe I'd look exactly like her." I laughed just a little.

"No," Ann said seriously. "It's more than that. It's something about the forehead and the cheekbones."

"Really?"

Beryl screwed her eyebrows together and

said, "Personally, I don't see it. Marylee is far prettier than this woman."

After class, when Johanna and I were drinking chamomile tea in my apartment, she said, "I agree with Beryl. I don't see a resemblance. You're much nicer looking than she is."

Later, after I'd been asleep for a whole lot of hours, something woke me. I sat up quickly, wondering if my car would start honking again, but no, it wasn't that. I turned on my bedside lamp and got up. When I turned on the light in my kitchen, I saw that the slide bolt to my French doors had been pulled back. I put my hand to my mouth and stared at it. I had closed this. I know I had; I was diligent about that. I remember distinctly pulling the bolt across. I examined the lock, then locked it again, and this time I put a little piece of masking tape across the end of it. It's not as if this would hold anything. But it might let me know if it had been tampered with, somehow. Maybe. I went back to bed, wondering if I should call the police. And what would I say? Someone came into my apartment and unlocked the door to my balcony?

"Was anything taken?"

"No."

And then the officers would look at me

and each other and try to hide their grins. I know this because this sort of thing had happened with my aunt on a regular basis.

SIX

Barbara's son Jared ended up being a tall, lanky guy, nice looking, who wore a button-down shirt with the sleeves rolled up at the elbows and brown corduroy pants. My first reaction was that he looked like a banker, the kind from old movies who wore bands around their upper arms and put on rubber fingers for counting money. He shook my hand like a gentleman, and Barbara and her husband, Harold, welcomed all of us and said grace and invited us to gather our food from the overladen dining-room table. We lined up on either side. I stood behind Johanna and found myself chatting happily with some of the women; Meredith and Ginger, and a petite pixie of a girl whose name I didn't get.

Meanwhile, on the other side of the table, Jared and a few of the guys talked about a new piece of spam-busting software.

I don't know how it happened, maybe

Barbara had something to do with it, but Jared and I ended up sitting next to each other on the love seat, just the two of us. We balanced plates of lasagna, hamburger casserole and baby-spinach salad on our laps, and he asked me how I liked living in Burlington.

"Fine," I said, my mouth stuffed with macaroni and cheese. Once I swallowed, I said, "It's nice here. I like it." Then I said, "Tell me what you did in Guatemala."

I have learned something in life — if you're the one who asks the questions, you don't have to answer any. I munched on a white roll, careful to keep casserole from spilling onto my lap while Jared talked. Johanna sat across from us on a hassock, and on the floor, people clustered around her feet like her minions. That was Johanna. People gathered around her in spite of themselves. I watched all of this while next to me Jared kept on talking. It dawned on me that I was only half listening and this made me feel awful. I caught myself even looking at his hands and comparing his fingers to Evan's. I shook my head to free that thought and Jared probably thought I was shaking my head at him.

"You don't agree with me?" he said.

I had no idea what he'd just said so I

smiled at him, smoothed my skirt and said, "I'm sorry, I was shaking my head on general principle. It had nothing to do with you."

And then, because I thought he deserved better, I asked him to tell me more about his trip. He did. And this time I made myself listen and found myself becoming interested. He spoke about villages lacking in necessities, no water or proper housing. He also told me he was nervous talking to groups, and didn't know how his presentation would go tonight. He had lots of pictures, he explained, but he was worried the computer wouldn't work. I told him he'd be fine. Jared had a gentle smile and his eyes were kind. A girl would be lucky to get him.

Barbara came in and grinned at the two of us sitting there and I knew what she was thinking.

Before dessert, his talk began. Jared kept nervously running the palms of his hands up and down the sides of his corduroy pants. For some reason I found the gesture annoying.

But when he launched into his speech, I became fascinated by the hardships in that country. A school for orphans was needed, and that's what Jared had signed on to do

— backbreaking construction work. He'd dug trenches in the heat, poured cement foundations, framed and painted.

After he finished answering the group's questions, he sat back down with me on the love seat. It was while I was whispering to Jared about what a great job he'd done that I noticed Evan was in the room. I don't know how long he'd been there, leaning backward on a kitchen chair, his legs hooked around the rungs, but when he saw me looking at him, he gave me a little finger wave.

I waved back.

". . . so now I'm back working on the police force."

"Pardon?"

Jared was talking to me. Again, my mind had been elsewhere.

"I was saying I was back at work now."

"Oh. Police work, right? You enjoy being back?"

He nodded and ran his hands again over his corduroy knees. "I guess I like helping people. Some things about it I don't like. Most I do."

I thought about something then. "Jared? Would you be able to do something for me?"

He had a crooked, cute way of smiling. "I can certainly try."

"It's kind of a police thing. But I haven't gone to the police with it, not yet, because it happened so long ago. It has to do with my parents. Their names were Allen and Sandra Simson and they died in a car accident here in Burlington."

"I'm sorry to hear that," he said softly.

"It's okay." I smiled up at him. "It happened when I was three. I don't even remember them."

"How did it happen?"

I hesitated. "I wish I knew. That's what I want to find out. I don't know what kind of a car accident it was. Like was there another car involved? Those are some of the questions I have. Would the police have records that go back that far?"

He looked at me for a long minute and I could tell what he was thinking — how is it that she doesn't know what happened to her own parents? "I'll do some checking around," he said. He wrote down the particulars on a piece of paper.

"Thanks," I said. Maybe this was a good thing, a God thing, even. I've heard that God puts you in places for a reason, and maybe that's why I'd come here tonight. Jared with his police connections could soon solve the mystery. And for all of my reticence about meeting him, he seemed to be a nice enough guy. I had no doubt that he would help me. Perhaps he'd even come up with an address, like the house I lived in when I was a baby. I'd meet family members. Maybe they still lived in the house. I'd also be able to find out why my aunt had spirited me off the way she had. *Thank you, Lord,* I silently prayed.

After the Bible study, Jared and I ended up being cornered by his parents. I didn't get to say goodbye to Johanna and I didn't see Evan leave, although I kept looking over my shoulder for him.

Back home in my apartment, I realized that I should have asked Jared about my French doors being unlocked. Maybe I should have even asked him about my car honking the way it had in the middle of the night. Since it had only happened that once, I'd paid it no more attention. Barbara had told me that the same thing had happened to her car and it ended up being a neighbor's cat. They finally figured it out when they saw the paw prints across the hood. None of this commonsense reasoning helped though. I kept thinking of the dark shadow I'd seen, the man looking up at me, my dreams, and wondered if my aunt had been right. There was something wrong here in Burlington, something evil. And maybe I should have stayed away. No, I countered myself, I had the police working for me now. Soon I would know. I *would* know! But I still didn't want to go to bed.

I sat in my living room in front of my quilting frame and picked up my needle. To rest my thoughts from all of this, I switched on the TV and found myself becoming involved in a hospital drama while I made miniscule stitches on the quilt. Maybe tonight I could finish this one small section of sky.

Quilting was something that I was learning the hard way, but I was determined to master it. And when I finished this quilt, I intended to display it in my shop as a tribute to her. I stitched, watched TV and thought about my aunt. This quilt was special. My aunt only completed half of this design of the Oregon coastline before she got too sick to continue.

I would be a liar if I said I never wondered if I really belonged to Aunt Rose in the first place. You hear of children being kidnapped and living for years with their captors. There was a time when I was a teenager that I'd truly believed that. But then I would look in the mirror. I have my aunt Rose's hair, her thin nose and lips that are barely there.

Even Johanna thought we looked alike.

Plus, Aunt Rose had been good to me, and kind. She'd taught me mirror arts and quilting, knitting and papermaking. She'd been so patient when I fumbled. "You are just like I used to be, Marylee, before I learned to sit still and work slowly, stitch by stitch. That's what it is, stitch by stitch." As I worked on matching stitch for stitch, the memories flooded my thinking.

The day I turned eight was the day my aunt Rose gave me the framed photo of my parents. That was also the day that I realized I was different.

To celebrate my birthday, my aunt Rose planned a swimming party. We had a small aboveground pool in our backyard. During hot weather, ours was the place to be. The day was full of sun and splashes and noise and water games. For my birthday my aunt had given me a rubber raft, which three of us could fit on. For hours my friends and I splashed and played on that thing, along with an assortment of other water toys, balls and water wings.

Long about the time the hot dogs were to be served I became conscious of a change in the air. It was one of those subtle things. One minute there was laughter, splashing and jumping in the pool, and the next moment there was silence. All seven girls were huddled on one reclining deck chair on the opposite side of the patio. I could see the direction of their eyes, first flitting to me, then to Aunt Rose and then back to me. More titters. More stares.

"Hey!" I called from the pool. "Come on!"

The water of the pool had settled and was like a rumpled mirror reflecting the sun like veins.

The girls didn't budge. "Hey!" I called. "Don't you guys want to swim?"

More titters, more whispers.

"What's the matter?" I looked helplessly at my aunt, who was arranging hot dogs on a plate. She didn't look at me. The big pink birthday cake she'd made gleamed in the sun. I climbed up the ladder and approached the cluster of girls who seemed to close ranks.

"What's the matter?" I said again, attempting to gentle my way into the huddle.

Nervous giggles.

I still did not give up. "Hey, you want to go swimming?"

Without a towel around my shoulders, I felt shivery and cold, and my teeth had started to chatter.

Still no answer.

Finally, one of the girls, a chubby one

named Lisa, stepped out toward me and said, "How come you don't have a dad? Or a mom?"

"Yeah, how come?" asked another.

"Yeah," said the rest of them.

"I have a mom," I said defensively. "I have a dad, too."

"Then where are they?"

"They died," I answered.

Aunt Rose called us to the table for lunch. The subject didn't come up for the rest of the afternoon. But as I watched the girls get picked up by mothers and fathers and sisters and brothers in cars, I realized for the first time just how different I was. And I didn't like this differentness. I didn't like what I was feeling.

After everyone had gone and we were back inside, my aunt Rose sat down beside me on the couch.

"It's about time you had this."

I looked down at the couple standing barefoot beside the lake.

"Your parents," she said. "This is the only picture I have left of your mother and father since the accident. You should have it." She laid the framed photo on my lap.

At this point I had no idea the importance this picture would have for me. I got up from the couch, hugging it close. "I need to show my friends," I said. "I'll show them, then they'll know. I really do have a mom and dad."

Around eleven, my fingers and eyes were sore from the close work, so I put my needle and thread away. I was still reluctant to go to bed. A cup of tea would hit the spot, I decided. While I waited for the kettle to boil, for the umpteenth time I went through the pictures my aunt's lawyer had sent. But nothing significant jumped out at me. I still couldn't figure out why my aunt had an account book from the store where she worked. I decided to go through it carefully, line by line, page by page. Who knows? Maybe there was something important there.

It was a standard ledger accounting book, entirely filled with small square pencil notations. I turned to the front of the book, but the page that would have identified the store and the place was torn out.

It was not in my aunt's handwriting. Along the top of each page were dates. It was the year before I moved with my aunt to Portland. So, did that mean this book was from Burlington? But if this book was from her Burlington days, why had she taken it with her to Portland, and then left it with her lawyer?

I bowed my head. *Dear God, help me to figure out what's important.*

Then I began. I skimmed page after page of the sort of inventory you might find in a Home Depot: pounds of nails, hammers, two-by-fours, screwdrivers and mirrors. Mirrors? I thought about that. I had assumed this was for her craft store. Obviously it wasn't.

I read through pages and pages of accounts receivable and cash-register amounts. A few of the pages had asterisks at the top in ink that looked as if they had been added later. I wondered why they were marked.

I drank my tea and read. Then, tired and yawning, finding nothing and barely able to keep my eyes open, I closed the book. I'd finish my perusal when I was more alert.

When I went to close the book, the back cover fell open. When I looked down at what was written in the inside, I put a hand to my mouth. This time I did recognize my aunt's writing.

A piece of paper looked as if it had been glued to the inside back cover. Along the top I read *Burlington Store Clerks,* and then a list of six names, none of which I recognized. One of the names had an asterisk in ink beside it.

I blinked at the name, Danny M. Smythe. I put my chin in my hand. Could he be related to Marty Smythe, the man in my class? But I dismissed that. Marty had not recognized the name Sandy and Allen Simson, when I'd asked him. I recognized none of the other names, but now I had a starting point and names to begin tracking down.

SEVEN

When you own and manage a craft store, or any kind of gift store for that matter, you are continually walking the fine line between clutter and cozy. And Crafts and More was veering dangerously close to the clutter end of the spectrum. I needed somehow to put the clutter and questions in my life on hold and take care of the clutter in my store. I hadn't slept much the previous night, plus the latte with the double shot of espresso wasn't really helping.

I'd spent most of the previous night going through my aunt's things again. Looking for pictures of my parents, I'd been through all the boxes of her crafts and personal items so many times that I knew all of the contents by heart. Now I was looking for something else, some references to a hardware store. But I found none. My aunt had succeeded in erasing all traces of my parents from our new life in Portland. I'd also used Google to search for the names written in the back of the ledger book. I found no matches for some and so many for others that I didn't know where to begin. I put the whole thing aside for now.

Yet this morning all of that needed to be put on hold while I cleaned and dusted. I also needed to take care of another item on my to-do list. I hadn't yet paid Evan for researching my picture. I got out my checkbook and wrote a check for what I thought might be a reasonable amount.

To Evan Baxter,
For services rendered.

Thank you for the information about the picture. If this isn't enough, please let me know.

Marylee

I enclosed the check and sealed the envelope. That should do it, I thought. I put a stamp on it and set it out for the mailman. That done, I decided to get back to my store.

Time to remove those cute little bric-a-brac dolls from the windowsills and put up some real art. Time to take down that tacky summer wreath from the window. I'd reserved the space between the front windows for a gorgeous handcrafted mirror my aunt had made. I also planned to get some of her quilts out of storage and on the walls. When I finished her full-sized quilt, I'd put that up, if I deemed it was good enough.

My aunt had handcrafted this perfectly round mirror, its edges decorated in broken pieces shaped like leaves. It was a beautiful thing that I'd had to bundle carefully between sheets of heavy cardboard and Styrofoam for my trip across the country from Portland. Because it was such a heavy and fragile thing, I needed my wits about me, plus all my tools to get it up securely and without any sort of mishap.

I dug out the mirror from its cardboard casing, got my toolbox and my stepladder, and carried all of these things to the front of my store. I climbed up nearly to the top of the ladder with my stud finder in hand. I was two rungs from the top of the stepladder when I heard a male voice. I started, turned. Evan?

It was Jared who stood there in full police uniform.

"Hey, Jared, hi."

"Anything I can help you with up there?"

"Great. Can you hand me that mirror?"

"Sure."

"Be careful. It's very fragile and heavier

than it looks."

"I could climb up there if you'd like, and help you get that up."

"That's okay," I said. A lot of people found it difficult to believe that Aunt Rose and I could do a lot of things that men normally do, like hammer nails, and put up cupboards and shelves, use a cordless drill and change a tire. Jared watched while I hit the stud the first time. Then I hefted the mirror and placed it against the wall.

"Really nice," Jared said when the mirror was firmly attached. I asked him if it was straight and he backed up and said it was round, so how could something round be straight?

I chuckled and said, "But do you think it looks good here or should it be on the wall above the cash register?"

He cocked his head and said, "I don't think it really matters. You and my mother, you're the ones with the eye for those sorts of things."

I stood beside him and looked at the mirror. It looked fine there. My little craft store already looked better because of it. Standing beside him, I realized just how tall he was, taller than Evan, but leaner and lankier, the sort of look you would get if you unraveled a coat hanger and stood it up on its end. Evan, on the other hand, seemed more solid. Stop it, I told myself. Stop comparing him to Evan.

After a while, Jared turned to me. "Marylee, I came here to see you because I have some bad news."

I blinked.

He hesitated before he said, "I ran your parents' names through the system this morning."

I leaned toward him. I could barely breathe.

"They aren't there."

I stared at him. "What do you mean they aren't there?"

"There's no record of a car accident killing a young couple in their thirties in Burlington in the year you specified. And just to be on the safe side, I checked three years on either side. Also, I couldn't find any DMV records for them either. Are you sure they lived here?"

I thought about the list of names in the back of the accounts book and said, "I'm sure. What about Rose Carlson?"

He shook his head. "Nothing on her, either."

"But there has to be something."

He shrugged. "I'm sorry. I don't know what to say about this."

But there has to be information, I wanted to scream at him. There just *has* to be.

He asked, "Have you been to city hall? They might have some property records."

"I've checked the cemeteries, a few anyway. There are a lot in Burlington, so it's taken some time. But going to city hall is a good idea." I tried to keep the desperation out of my voice. I knew it was Burlington. I'd seen the proof in my aunt's own handwriting, hadn't I? Suddenly I felt tired. The late night was catching up with me and all the double espresso was doing was making me jittery.

"Marylee, I'm really sorry. I know this means a lot to you."

It took me a few seconds to realize that he'd reached for me and was now holding my hand.

"It's okay," I said, drawing my hand back. "Everything about this place is a mistake. I should never have come here."

He regarded me sadly. "I don't think it's a mistake that you're here."

EIGHT

Two days later I spoke with Evan. I don't open until noon on Saturdays, so that morning, I ordered my usual latte, not a double this time, and took a seat at a small table by the window with a brochure for the Vermont Quilt Festival. Across the street, the cat in the window of the mystery bookstore lazily swished his tail. I tried reading, but couldn't concentrate. I needed something to settle my mind. Yesterday I'd discovered that I wasn't a real person.

City hall had no record of Sandra and Allen Simson ever owning property in Burlington. Later I'd gotten out my birth certificate. Yes, my name was listed as Marylee Simson and my parents were Sandra and Allen. By phone I'd checked with the department of records. And what I'd found had shocked me. No record of Marylee Simson being born in Burlington.

That made me afraid. Was my birth certificate a fake? I thought about marching into the office with it, proving to them that I was real, showing this to them, but decided against it. That act might unleash a whole string of stuff I might not be prepared to deal with. Like who was I? And what was I doing wandering through life with phony papers?

I'd leave well enough alone, at least for the time being. Maybe the answers lay with the picture. I needed to swallow my pride and go back to see Evan with the picture again.

I was thinking about this when suddenly Evan was sitting across from me.

He plunked the check I'd sent him down on the table between us. "There's something wrong with this check."

I picked it up, peered at it. The date was correct. I'd signed it. Had the bank refused it because they'd finally figured out that I wasn't who I thought I was? That alarm must've shown in my face because Evan said gently, "Hey, it's okay. I was kidding. The check's fine. I'm just not going to cash it."

"Why not?"

"I only accept payment when I've written up an invoice. It flubs up my computer program."

I looked up. "But you did a job for me." I hadn't noticed before how long his hair was, and how it curled not only over his forehead, but over his shirt collar. The collar of his blue shirt was bunched under the lapel of his green canvas jacket. I fought the urge to reach over and straighten it for him.

"Well," he said, leaning back and crossing his arms over his chest, "I won't be cashing this check. It's way too much anyway. I'd never charge this much to examine a picture."

He pushed his glasses up on his nose and went on. "This is not why I came to see you. I came in here today to talk to you because of something else, something I need to apologize for. I hope I didn't embarrass you too much by winking in the morning."

I looked at him. "No, uh, that was okay. I wasn't embarrassed, really," I stammered, feeling my ears get warm.

"Here's why I'm here." He placed his palms on the table. "I noticed you in this shop a few months ago. There was something about you, even then, that was different. So, I made it my business to get to know who you were and where you came from. I asked around and learned that you were the new person in town who'd bought the craft store, which was, I must say, pretty badly run by those elderly sisters. You've brought life into the place. You've done a remarkable job. Everyone says so. And then when you came into my shop . . ." His voice trailed off. "So, of course, I was a bit disappointed when you wouldn't go to dinner with me. But now I know why. Wrongheadedness on my part, and I apologize for that."

I looked at him. Wrongheadedness? About what? I scrunched up my eyes and looked at him.

"But all you needed to do was to say that you were seeing someone else. I would've understood." He was grinning now, trying to make me feel comfortable.

"What?" I leaned forward and looked at him squarely. "What're you talking about?"

"I'm talking about you and Jared. You must be happy now that he's back home safe and sound."

Oh, dear. Oh, dear. Oh, dear.

He went on. "Jared seems like a really nice guy. I only met him that once. His father, Harold, bought a camera from me recently. It was Harold who invited me to the dinner so I could meet Jared. Nice guy. Nice group."

I needed him to stop. I put up my hand. "Evan. Wait. I'm not seeing Jared. That night at the dinner was the first time I ever laid eyes on him."

He stopped, regarded me, the beginnings of a grin at the corners of his mouth. "Really?"

"Really," I said.

"But I thought, I mean his mother works at your store. I thought, how cozy and nice that is. And it looked like you guys were old pals."

Oh, dear. Double oh, dear. "I'm not seeing Jared."

And then I watched the corners of his mouth go down in the beginnings of a concentrated frown. I could almost see the wheels turning. He was probably wondering if there was another reason why I'd turned him down. Maybe I owed him an explanation. "Why I left in such a hurry that morning has nothing to do with you," I said. "It has to do with me. I should have said no and given you my reasons like an ordinary person."

"You don't owe me any reasons," he said, obviously hoping I had good, safe ones.

But I do, I thought. And the reason is that Johanna is in love with you and I don't want to hurt her. Instead I blurted out, "It's because . . . It's because I was engaged once. It turned out badly. I'm just not ready."

I really don't know why I said it. It wasn't foremost on my mind, but there it was.

He didn't respond for a while. Then he said, "So was I. Once a long time ago. It hurts, doesn't it? Is that why you always look so sad?"

I didn't answer him. I didn't even know how to begin answering him. That wasn't it at all. I had long ago fallen out of love with my ex-fiancé. I was sad and hurt and confused because of so many other reasons that had nothing to do with Mark.

My reasons had to do with being lied to by my aunt Rose. They had to do with not knowing who my parents were or how they died. They were about feeling lost and family-less in a world where everyone was surrounded by brothers and sisters.

They had to do with not even knowing who I was.

Those were the things that I couldn't tell Evan. It wasn't about Mark at all. The fiasco of my engagement merely provided a convenient excuse when asked, "What's wrong?"

He took a drink of his coffee, set down the mug and looked at my quilting brochure. He said, "My sister made a beautiful quilt once. I have it hanging in my house."

"You have a sister who quilts?" I asked. "Really?"

"Used to. Do you have a quilting frame?"

I was surprised he even knew what a quilting frame was. "I do," I said. "My aunt gave me one when I graduated. It takes up most of my living room."

"That's what I like, a living room that's useful. Reason I ask about the quilting frame is that I think there's an old one kicking around my parents' basement. I could find out what they plan to do with it."

"Your sister doesn't quilt anymore?"

"No . . ."

Around us the coffee shop was noisy, but something had happened to Evan's eyes when he'd mentioned his sister. We toyed with our coffee for a while, and I think he may have found the silence uncomfortable because he said, "I just want you to know that the offer is always open. If you want Mose and me to have another look at the picture, just drop it by. And we don't even have to go to dinner together." He winked at me. "I may have a few more ideas."

"Thank you," I said. "Maybe I'll take you up on that."

"This picture must mean a lot to you."

I took a deep breath, considered. I may as well tell him, since so many other people knew. "It's of my parents. Or, I think it's my parents. I don't know for sure." And then I told him a bit about my history, how they'd died in a car accident and how I'd left Burlington shortly after that to live with my aunt.

He was leaning forward, his hands on the table, listening as I shared with him. "I would consider it an honor to help you," he finally said. "And just to let you know, I won't be sending you an invoice. You are a friend. I don't charge friends."

"Friends," I said.

"Just friends," he added.

Nine

If there were a problem with the name Marylee Simson, I would have known by now. I've been filing my income taxes for a whole lot of years with no problems, no glitches, not even a question. I even established a business under that name, took out a loan. So, no, there's nothing wrong with who I am. Just some foul-up at the Department of Records here in Vermont, some inept file clerk at the government. And besides, I had a shop to run.

I work six days a week at Crafts and More. I have to, to make a go of it and be semi-successful. I give three craft classes, two in the evening — mirror arts and quilting — and a seniors' scrapbooking class in the afternoon down at the seniors' center. Sunday is basically my only day off, but I can easily spend Sunday afternoons on Crafts and More business if I let myself. Barbara is always telling me I need to spend some time off, so after church when Johanna asked me to go to a fall craft fair in the afternoon and then meet up with two girls I'd recently met at church, Meredith and Ginger, for supper and a movie, at first I balked. Too busy. Too much to do. I had a fall sale coming up and I was way behind in the planning of it. Plus, I had ordering to do and bills to pay. But then I could almost hear Barbara's voice: "Crafts and More is becoming you and you are becoming Crafts and More, and that's not good, Marylee."

So I decided to go. It was a craft fair after all. And I run a craft store, right? So it was almost like working. Burlington's biggest craft fairs are held in the summer, but all during the fall and leading up to Christmas there are craft fairs practically every weekend all over the city. The one we were going to was being held at the center where I give my seniors' scrapbooking class.

Just before three, Johanna pulled into my back alley to pick me up. Two minutes after I climbed into her passenger seat, she looked at me sternly and said, "I've been doing some thinking."

"That's dangerous."

"No, Marylee, I'm serious. I have to tell you this right off. Not only do I think it's okay for you to go out with Evan, now I think you *should* go out with him."

"Johanna. I have no intention of —"

"Here's what I know," she interrupted, jangling her hand at me. Literally. She was wearing lots of colored bangly metal bracelets today. "I saw the way he was looking at you at Barbara and Harold's. He couldn't take his eyes off you. Okay, I admit it, I would love it if he could look at me that way, but that's not happening, so here it is, and I mean this. If you want to be with Evan, you have my blessing. I don't want this to come between our friendship in any way."

"Johanna, I told you, I'm not interested. Evan and I are just friends."

She continued her hand waggling at me. "So you say, but I see the way you look at him, too. There's no denying that." She shook her head. "I would truly love it if you two ended up together. That's all I'm saying."

"That's not going to happen."

"It'll happen," she said. "I've made peace with the whole thing." She turned her full attention back to her driving.

I sighed loudly and theatrically.

Johanna glanced over but didn't say anything.

A few minutes later she pulled into the

crowded parking lot of the seniors' center. I was looking forward to the craft fair, which probably shows how boring I am, that I can get excited over a craft fair. But I like good ones, and yes, I could see when we entered the large room that had been transformed into many little boutiques that this was a good one.

The place was loud, festive and crowded. We examined pottery, watercolor paintings, handmade cards and paper, jewelry, lengths of cloth and painted wooden toys. We draped ourselves with handwoven shawls, which were kind of pricey, but gorgeous. I would have loved one, and ended up taking the weaver's business card. Things aren't exactly tight financially at the store, but I want to make sure I have a cushion.

In addition to being extremely creative, Aunt Rose was also a good money manager. Here is her theory: Whatever percent you tithe and give to charity, that was the amount you put in your savings account. It's something I still do. Which was why I put back the woven shawls and walked past the hand-tooled purses that looked like the ones you see with designer labels.

Johanna bought armloads of handcrafted toys for various nieces and nephews, and a necklace for a twelve-year-old niece. I bought a set of dangly earrings with tiny blue stars from the same jeweler, my one purchase at the fair.

When you got right down to it, the reason that I'm able to save money is probably because I have no one to buy for. This was the first Christmas I'd be totally on my own. Last year it was just after my aunt had died and I'd spent the holidays with my former fiancé's huge extended family. I had plenty of people to buy for last year and there had been lots of gifts for me under the tree, as well. I'd felt welcome and at home with them. This year was different. Except I couldn't help but think of how Evan would look in that Irish fisherman's sweater.

When I'd made the decision to come out here, I hadn't thought about things like Christmas. Johanna seemed to pick up on this, and while we were sitting at an indoor picnic table at the concession end of the craft fair drinking not-too-good coffee out of little foam cups, she said to me, "I know it's not for a few months, Marylee, but I have an invitation for you. This comes from my mother and my sisters. We all want you to know that you are invited to spend Christmas with us. We'll drive over to Montpelier on Christmas Eve. They live in this huge old farmhouse with about a hundred extra rooms. I have to warn you, it's kind of crazy though. My three married brothers and all their kids always come and then my two sisters, plus I've got a zany assortment of aunts and uncles. On Christmas Eve we always go to the church service, and then it's back home for desserts, which are totally to die for, everything you can imagine, and then in the morning there's Christmas stockings for everyone, and then there are presents under the tree. And of course no Christmas Day would be complete without the afternoon game of charades. It's sort of a tradition at our house."

Before she could even come up for air I said, "I'd love to come." And I meant it.

We threw our empty cups away. It was almost time to meet Meredith and Ginger at the restaurant and then it would be off to the movie, which Johanna had described as "a sweeping historical-time-travel-love-story-chick-flick."

On the way out, I saw Marty and Dot bent over a display of stained-glass windcatchers. Marty looked up and I waved happily. He grinned and waved. "Johanna," I said, "you have to meet these friends of mine.

"Hey, Marty," I called. "Getting a head start on your Christmas shopping already?"

"Sure are," he said, patting Dot's hand.

"Aren't we, love?"

"We are, love," she said.

"You need to have a display of your own quilts here, Marylee," he told me. "You could sell lots."

"Maybe next year," I said. "Too busy this year. Marty, Dot, meet my friend Johanna."

I introduced everyone and the four of us stood at the entryway and chatted comfortably for a while. Marty took a handkerchief out of his pocket and wiped his brow then, and I felt it again, that feeling, that something was wrong. I looked over at Marty and Dot, at their smiles, especially Dot's, and something about the way his hand lingered on Dot's shoulder chilled a place deep inside of me. And I had absolutely no idea why.

I needed to think. I needed to get away somewhere to think. Unfortunately for me, that isn't an option, being tied to Crafts and More the way I am. I don't even have the luxury of a solitary cubicle office. No, each morning I'm required to go downstairs with my nicest, most cheerful shopkeeper's smile. Even when people complain that they could get the same thing elsewhere for half the price, I have to smile and nod and talk about personal service, classes and money-back guarantees.

But this afternoon, after I closed the shop for the day, I decided to go for a long walk, my equivalent to getting away. As soon as I hung the Closed sign on the door and brought in my flag, I ran upstairs, changed into jeans and a sweater, and headed out. This time, instead of walking along the waterfront, I got into my car and parked at North Beach. There were a whole lot of trails and paths here that I hadn't explored. The sun hung low in the sky like a red ball over the water when I set out. It was gorgeous. Leaves that remained on the trees glowed golden. I walked past joggers and cyclers and mothers pushing strollers.

I thought about how much Aunt Rose would have liked a day like today. I'm a walker because she walked. The shop in Portland where she'd worked was four miles from our home, and she'd walked to and from work every day no matter the weather. In my mind I could see her fast stride, the way she swung her arms, her pointed nose, the seriousness of her demeanor.

I'd walked almost a mile when I heard a voice behind me. "Marylee! Hey, Marylee!"

I turned. Evan? He was grinning and sprinting toward me in track pants and jogging shoes.

"Here I am out on my daily run and who do I see but you?"

"Hi," I said.

"But you do walk quickly. I could barely catch up and I'm running."

"I guess I do," I answered. "It comes from growing up with an aunt who walked everywhere she went.

"Do you always jog here?" I asked.

He pushed his glasses up on his nose. "It's my favorite place."

"Well, it's beautiful."

"Can I join you on your walk?"

"Sure. Okay." I wasn't interested in Evan. No, not the least little bit. And the fact that my heart seemed to be beating out of my chest, that had nothing to do with anything. I was glad I was wearing my sunglasses. He wouldn't be able to see me helplessly staring at his face like some lost puppy.

"Walking's good," he said. "Good exercise. Almost as good as running. Less hard on the knees."

"For my aunt it wasn't exercise, it was merely a way to get from point A to point B. It was her thrifty nature. She never drove if where we were going was within a couple of miles. When I was a teenager I used to die of embarrassment by the fact that we were like the only people in the entire county who walked to church on Sundays. I used to hope that none of my friends would see me walking with my aunt. And now I'm just like her." As we walked, I looked at him closely. "You got a haircut." I missed that little piece that fell across his forehead. I didn't tell him that, though.

"Oh that." He ran his hand self-consciously through his hair. "Thought it was about time. I get so forgetful of things like my hair. It was my mom who finally convinced me to get it cut. I've got a showing of my photographs at some fancy gallery in a week so I guess I need to look presentable."

I stopped. "You have a showing in a gallery?"

"Yep. I'm not crazy about those things. Everybody all dressed up in suits, walking around eating and getting schmozzed on free alcohol and trying not to spill things and trying to look oh so sophisticated about art."

"But, Evan, that's quite an honor. I'm truly impressed." I thought about the pictures I'd seen hanging in his shop; the one of the little girl, her face lit with the light of a campfire, the way he'd captured the blues of the fire, even the greens. I thought about the photo of the quilts, the wedding pictures that weren't quite like any wedding pictures I'd ever seen before. "Your pictures are quite artistic, really good."

"Thank you. It's something I enjoy."

We were climbing down on the rocks now and he took my hand. I liked how that felt. I was pleased that he held on just a bit longer than he needed to, and was disappointed when he let go.

We chatted easily then, about crafts and art, and I mentioned the craft fair I'd recently gone to.

"Didn't you know? *Craft Fair* is Burlington's middle name."

"I'm beginning to realize this."

We'd gone maybe half a mile up the rugged shoreline when Evan stopped abruptly, nearly causing me to fall into him, which wouldn't have been a bad thing, and said, "That building!"

"What?"

"Do you see that light? The way the sun is reflecting off the tin roof of that old building? Like a mirror." Evan was scrambling over rocks, and I followed along. "I love that particular color of the setting sun," he added. Out of an inner pocket, he produced a tiny digital camera.

"You brought a camera out jogging?"

"Never leave home without it," he said

and winked at me. He stilled and aimed the camera at the corner of the building. It was an old boathouse he was so excited about, a sagging, wooden structure that he scrambled around, stopping, aiming his camera toward, then scurrying to another location. The building looked as if the city fathers had somehow missed it when they set about to revitalize the lakefront. It had a big garage door in the front, a small door in the back, one filmy, greasy window, and a roof made of tin.

"The colors," I said, "remind me of the picture you have on your wall of the little girl and the campfire."

"I find the colors of fire so fascinating. I like contrasts. I like them in colors, a hot campfire on a dark winter night. I also like contrasts in subject matter — the unhappy bride, the jubilant street person. I love this old boathouse," he said. "I've been trying for a long time to get the light just right. You might just be my lucky charm." He winked at me. "I'll have to bring you along more often."

I followed him, fascinated, not only with him, but with his artistic vision. It was as if when he was doing his art he had no eyes, no thoughts for anything or anyone else, except his art. I could just as well have been a grain of sand on the shore. While other women might find this disconcerting, I found it refreshing. It was difficult not to compare him to my ex-fiancé whose eyes had routinely glazed over when I mentioned quilt patterns.

I studied his hands, the way they held the tiny camera. "I should have my bigger SLR so I could change lenses," he said. "I should go get it, but by the time I got it, this remarkable fire-like quality would be gone. Look at the way it shimmers on the cornice of that building."

I didn't answer. He wasn't talking to me. I knew that. I often talk to myself when I'm working on a new design or arranging mirror pieces just so. He knelt and aimed repeatedly until the sun set.

"Not perfect. But good," he said, putting his camera in his pocket. "I'll take these back to my computer and see what I've come up with."

"Can I see them?" I asked.

"You want to see them?" He seemed surprised that I would ask this.

"I'd love to."

We stood close together as he flipped through the photos on the little camera screen. I was surprised that he had taken so many in the few moments we'd scrambled around the building. I saw the light like a fire burning above the building, reflecting a brackish radiance off the roof. He had captured more, if possible, than had actually been there to begin with.

"These are good," I said. My hand brushed his. "These are really good." We were standing so close and I didn't want the moment to end, and maybe if I kept talking, admiring his work, it didn't have to. But even as we stood there the light was fading and a chill was making its way through my thin sweater. I shivered.

"What about warming up someplace? Getting a bite to eat? You up for that?"

"That might be nice." I smiled at him. "My car's back in the parking lot."

"So's mine. Here, take my jacket."

He took off his big hoodie and draped it around my shoulders. It was soft and warm and smelled like him.

"I could have managed," I protested.

"I'll be fine. This shirt's made of a special wicking material that keeps me warm. In fact, I was getting too hot."

I didn't believe him but took the arm he offered gratefully as we continued. We were the only people walking along the beach this time of the evening, yet to my left I heard footfalls and stopped.

"What's the matter?" Evan asked.

"I thought I heard something."

"An animal most likely. There are lots around."

"But it sounded like a person walking."

We were on our way again, but I had the feeling, that crawly feeling that we were being followed, although that was surely impossible. I thought about the feeling that I'd had at that first mirror-arts class when I'd felt a black shadow pass. I thought about the man I'd seen looking up at my apartment. I kept looking over and saw no one. My imagination. It had to be. I'd inherited this paranoia from my aunt. Yet, this evening, the feeling was so pronounced it *had* to be real.

"Someone's following us. I can feel it," I finally said.

He looked at me. "Should I check, just to be sure?"

I nodded. It was too dark now and the chill penetrated Evan's hoodie. We were too far from our cars on a lonely stretch of beach. "Maybe it's a deer," I offered.

Evan produced a small flashlight and shone it into the trees. We saw no one.

"You brought a flashlight?" I whispered.

"I'm an old Boy Scout and why are you whispering?"

"I have no idea why I'm whispering." I kept whispering.

"You're also shivering. It's probably an animal, maybe a stray cat. Let's get to our cars. You need to seriously warm up."

Later on, in a little restaurant with our hands around mugs of hot coffee, I began to feel a little less spooked, a little less chilled. I even asked Evan to tell me more about his photography, and he talked happily about cameras, digital versus print, and how he had worked as an accountant for two years but then decided to take the plunge and try to make a living doing what he loved the most. I ate my veggie burger and sweet-potato fries and mostly listened. He seemed to enjoy his ribs and a baked potato. He was easy to talk to and I found myself relaxing in his presence. I could understand the attraction Johanna had for him. And despite what I'd originally thought about him, his lack of commitment, his unceremonious dropping of Johanna, I found myself, like Johanna, making excuses for him. Maybe it was the way his eyes screwed up when he laughed.

Over dessert I brought up the subject of my parents again. I told him that I'd found out that no one by their names had owned property or been in a car accident in Burlington. I told him about the ledger book I'd found and the six names under the heading Burlington Store Clerks.

"So now I think I might be in the right place and then I find that there's no police record of a fatal accident occurring at that time. And two people dying in a collision would have been significant. So now I'm wondering if I'm in the right place again. I don't even know who I am." I stopped, just short of telling him that there was no record of me being born here. I don't know why but I felt I should keep this fact to myself for a while. I said, "Maybe I have no family anywhere. Maybe my real mother dropped me off on a church doorstep and Rose Carlson took me in and adopted me and then made up this whole dramatic story of my life."

"That doesn't make sense," Evan said gently. "If that were the case, why wouldn't your aunt change your name to hers?"

"Maybe it's part of the whole charade." I felt tears well in the corners of my eyes. I swiped at them with my fist. "I loved my aunt. She was all that I had. But I get so mad at her for dying without telling me anything!"

The tears, which a few moments ago had only threatened, were now full-blown and coursing down my cheeks. I hated to be this way in front of Evan. "Maybe my whole life is a lie," I said.

"Your life is not a lie." He reached forward as if he was going to touch my face. He seemed to change his mind in midstream and he cupped the candle holder in the middle of the table. "No one's life is a lie," he said. "No one is here by accident. You're not even here in Burlington by accident. God has a plan in all of this."

"Well, I wish I knew what it was! I wish my aunt would have told me more about me!"

He seemed thoughtful for a moment and said, "You said your aunt sent you an old accounts book? Maybe I could have a look at it. Would you mind?"

"You've done so much for me already."

"I'm happy to do this for you. I consider it a challenge."

I hesitated. I had another reason for not wanting him to do this. I didn't want to surrender the book. So I said, "Maybe I could show it to you. We could work on it together."

"How about right now?"

I regarded him. "Now?"

"No time like the present. I know this is a concern for you, Marylee. And the quicker we can resolve this issue, the quicker you'll be able to get on with your life."

"Well, we could go over to my store," I said. "I've got this big table in a back room. I could spread out the pictures for you, too. You could have a look at them."

"Well —" he got up and extended his hand to help me up "— let's get started."

Forty-five minutes later I was going through the pictures for the umpteenth time, and Evan's head was bent over the ledger book. He made notes on a piece of paper beside him.

"I think we might have something here," he said finally.

I looked up from the photos.

"These asterisks," he said. "Did you notice that this one name has an asterisk beside it? It's the only name with an asterisk."

I had noticed that.

"There are a few pages in the book with this same asterisk in pen at the top." I bent my head to see where he was pointing.

"I've looked carefully at these pages and you know what I found?" His eyes were bright.

"What did you find?"

"Discrepancies."

"Explain." I came over to his side of the table.

"Okay, here's what I think. Each of these pages represents a day in the life of this store, whatever this store was called. We can see it sold hardware items, but we don't know exactly what it was or where it was located. What I do know is on these days, the ones with the asterisk in ink at the top, the cash in hand at the end of the day doesn't match the money made in sales for that day."

"So, someone was embezzling from the store?"

"That's my guess. And then I look to the back here, at these pasted-in names. This name, Danny Smythe, has an asterisk beside it. Perhaps there is a connection."

I said, "Perhaps this Danny Smythe knows something about the discrepancies here."

"Or perhaps Danny Smythe is the one responsible for the cash shortfall."

I put my head in my hands. "Martin Smythe is a lovely old gentleman who attends one of my classes with his lady friend. I asked him, asked the whole class if they recognized the names Allen and Sandy Simson, but no one did."

"Why would you assume these names and this store have anything to do with your parents?"

I nodded, thought about it for a while,

and offered, "Because this is my aunt's handwriting?"

"Maybe it has more to do with your aunt than your parents," he offered.

We searched Danny Smythe on Google and found a bunch of places to look, but none that we could see had anything to do with hardware stores in Burlington.

He asked if he could take the book with him and I said yes. By this time it was late, and Evan said he needed to get back. "Four-thirty comes awful early," he told me with a grin.

I looked at him wide-eyed. "You get up at four-thirty?"

"No. I'm just saying it comes awful early."

"Oh, you," I said.

We stood at my door for a while before he said goodbye, my heart beating fast. I wondered if he would kiss me, but he looked at me, touched my cheek with his hand and said, "Good night, Marylee. Tomorrow? At the coffee shop? I'll be the one doing the winking."

TEN

I thought he would call. Well, wouldn't you expect a guy to call after a nice evening like the one I described? But the following morning he wasn't at the coffee shop. All day he didn't call. Around noon I sent him a cheery "Hello, how are you?" e-mail. Every spare minute I'd race to the back of my shop and check my e-mail, but nothing. Well, I should have known. Look what he did to Johanna. Why did I think he would be any different with me?

I managed to get through my mirror-arts class the following night, still expecting Evan to call at any minute. After class I even told Johanna. "We had a really nice walk and dinner. Really romantic." But even as I said it, I felt an inkling of anxiousness about the whole thing. I didn't need this, I told myself during the evening, which I spent quilting and watching an old movie. I really did not need this. And did I ask Marty about Danny Smythe? I did not. I guess I was waiting for Evan to do that, or maybe it was that I didn't think about Marty, when I wondered, and even worried, about Evan.

On the second day that Evan didn't call I began to get nervous about my aunt's accounting book. Why did I ever let him take it?

On the third night with no word from Evan, I called Johanna and invited her over. "We need to commiserate," I said when she dropped in with a huge bouquet of fall mums. I told her all about our walk and our dinner, and the fact that Evan had now disappeared off the face of the planet. But it was my own fault, I said. I'd known better. Hadn't I told her what kind of a guy Evan was? And look, this proved it.

We were sitting cross-legged on my living-room floor, eating microwaved popcorn out of a big bowl. And while I went on about this, Johanna leaned forward and aimed a popcorn kernel at me. "It's his fear of commitment. That's all this is about, Marylee. He was hurt so badly he's gun-shy, you know. That engagement. His fiancée just walked off. That's what I heard."

"Everybody gets hurt, Johanna," I said. "I'm sick of that being everybody's excuse."

She grabbed another handful of popcorn,

popped it in her mouth and said, "Why don't you go see him, then? Find out?"

"Oh yeah, right. Go see him. Good idea, Johanna."

"Go by his shop. He owes you, Marylee."

"He doesn't owe me."

"Sure he does. He almost kissed you."

"But he didn't kiss me. That's why he doesn't owe me." I picked up my mug of tea. "If he'd actually kissed me, then he'd owe me. But he didn't, so he doesn't. The rules."

"If he doesn't owe you for that, he owes you because he took your book, right?" She picked up another handful of popcorn. "So, now you have an excuse. You could go over there and ask him if he found anything else."

"I don't need an excuse to go over there. If I wanted to go over there, I just would."

"Then do it."

"Maybe I just will." I laughed.

"You should," she said, aiming another kernel at me. "So," she said, unwinding her legs, "what did you guys find in the book? You said he thought it might have something to do with your parents?"

I nodded. "Wait here. Let me get refills," I said, hopping up and carrying an empty Diet Coke bottle to the kitchen. On my way I noticed something near my front door. A sprinkling of white dust on the floor. Not much. In fact, if I hadn't looked down I wouldn't have even seen it. I bent down, fingered it. I looked up and above me it seemed little bits of ceiling were flaking onto the floor.

"Oh great," I called to Johanna. "Not only is my life falling apart, but my apartment is, too."

I sighed as I grabbed another bottle from the fridge. What was I even doing here in the first place? Was this whole building nothing but a run-down shack that was just moments away from falling? Had it been a colossal mistake buying it? Coming here at all? I was beginning to think so.

I told Johanna about the names and the asterisks and the name Danny Smythe when I returned with more drinks. "I've looked up Smythe in the phone book. There are too many, and no Dannys or Daniels."

"Where's that laptop of yours, Sherlock? We have work to do, my friend."

"The kitchen," I called after her, but she had already made her way in there. She was hitting keys even before she settled herself on the floor in front of me. "I mean, a quick Google search might not yield much, but it's a starting place. Your aunt writes *Burlington Store Clerks* and then a list — that's got to mean something."

"I already did that," I told her. "So did Evan."

"Well, we'll do it again. I know a better search engine. And you said you're sure that it was your aunt's handwriting?"

"Maybe. I don't know." I threw up my hands. "I'm not sure about anything anymore."

Later in the evening, after we'd unsuccessfully gone through many search engines, I asked her, "How do you really feel about Evan, Johanna? Have you moved on? Be totally honest, because at this point, I really don't care."

My fickle friend looked thoughtfully at me before she responded. "Yes," she said finally. "I can say that I've moved on. I mean I understand the attraction of Evan. He is so gorgeous. I mean, everyone will admit that, but I've given the whole thing to the Lord. I really have. If God has someone out there for me, well, that would be nice, but if not, so be it. And I shall be a wonderful aunt to my nieces and nephews and I'll be the best college teacher in the world."

"You'll find someone, Johanna. You are the coolest person I know."

"I'm too weird for most guys." She leaned back. "Did I tell you I'm thinking of going for my Ph.D.? In English lit. I've already talked to someone who wants to be my faculty adviser."

"Hey, that's really great, Johanna. I say go for it."

We made another batch of popcorn and talked about the pros and cons of higher education. We talked about guys and our dreams, which led us to settle comfortably on the couch to watch a sappy love story I'd rented, which had both of us in tears by the end.

The following day when I still hadn't heard from Evan, I decided to take Johanna's advice and go and see him. On my way to the seniors' center for my class, I'd stop in. What could it hurt? He had my book after all, right?

It was back to pouring rain, so I decided to drive instead of walk. I parked along the side of Evan's building, but his car wasn't there. What did that mean? I didn't know.

Two women were in the shop talking about video cameras to a small mousy man with longish rumpled hair whose name tag informed the world that he was Mose. So, this was the famous assistant. I stood by the counter and craned my neck to see if Evan was in a back room. Oh, forget this, I thought and went around the counter and stood in the doorway of the office. No Evan. And a wooden coat tree, I noticed, held only one coat. Mose's?

Framed photographs were stacked against a far wall. For the art show, I figured. On the desk was a computer and stacks of papers leaning into it. On a far desk was another computer with a large flat-screen monitor. I wondered if this was where Evan did his photo manipulation.

There were several closed doors, and I presumed one or more of them led to a darkroom. I turned. Mose was standing right behind me. He looked dusty, rather as if he had walked through a hallway of cobwebs.

"Hey," he said. "Is there something I can help you with?"

"I'm looking for Evan Baxter."

"He's not here."

"You're his assistant, Mose."

"Yes, I'm Mose." He bowed slightly from the waist.

"Nice to meet you," I said. "I'm Marylee."

"Yes," he said. "I know who you are."

"Do you know where Evan is?"

"He's visiting his sister."

"Do you know when he'll be back from visiting his sister?"

"Two more days. That's what he said in an e-mail."

An e-mail. He could write Mose an e-mail, but not me.

"Can you give me a number where he can be reached? Like, does he have a cell phone?"

"No," he said.

"No?" No cell phone? I didn't believe he didn't have a cell phone. *Children* have cell phones. I was mad and hurt and infuriated with myself for allowing my emotions, my attraction to the guy, to get out of hand.

"No," Mose said. "He has a cell phone, but I'm not at liberty to give out the cell phone number. I can't betray that confidence."

I walked out fuming. He *can't betray that confidence.* Well, what about me? I was betrayed big-time. He stole my book. For all I knew he'd dropped it in the middle of Lake Champlain off the ferry and I'd never see it again!

This was my ex all over again, I thought as I huffed my way out of the store. I slammed my car into gear and thought about all the times that he had stood me up. He hadn't been there for me after my aunt had died. Well, he had been at first. He'd held me when I'd cried into his chest and pounded my fist on the wall.

But it had soon grown old for him when after two months I couldn't look at my wedding magazines or talk about where we wanted to live or how many children I wanted. He'd roll his eyes and end our date when I fell into a crying jag and couldn't stop. "Get over it," he would demand of me. "Just get over it. Get over it, get over it, get over it."

I'd tried. I'd be good for a while. But then something would trigger it, the smell of her chocolate-chip cookies, the sight of a hand-stitched quilt on a clothesline, and I'd stand where I was and weep.

And then, finally, he "couldn't take it anymore" and he'd given me the last and irrevocable ultimatum: "You choose, Marylee. It's me or your dead aunt. You choose."

It was a relief later that afternoon to be in the company of people who liked me. I looked forward to seeing Marty and Dot and Muriel and the other seniors at the scrapbooking class. What I like most about this class is learning about their lives and listening to their stories. These people have so much wisdom, so much living behind them, so much to offer me.

Today I would try a different tack. I'd

show them the picture of my parents to see if any of them recognized them. No one in my mirror-arts class knew who they might be, but the people in my scrapbooking class had lived here longer. I would also mention the names I could remember from the back of the accounting book. That was worth a try, too.

At the common room of the center, I unloaded my supplies for the class. A woman named Jayne had asked me to bring some wide pink grosgrain ribbon. I didn't know the precise shade she wanted so I'd brought along all the shades of pink that I sold. I laid them out on the table along with various shades of paper ribbons and construction paper, bits and pieces of embroidery thread, yarn and fabric swatches. While I did this, Maddie set out the coffee. She was the pale young woman who manned the phones at the center. In addition to providing a room for seniors' activities, and despite its name, this building also housed the Boys and Girls Club, a room for teen after-school activities and a day care. Before Maddie, I had never seen anyone with white-blond eyelashes. Yet her personality was anything but pale. While I put out my wares, she plugged in the coffeepot and set out the foam cups and powdered cream and sugar packets.

"We're so happy you're doing this," she said as she bustled about. "Everybody just raves about this class."

I grinned and told her I got as much out of it as the seniors did. This was the only class I didn't charge for. Plus, I gave them a hearty senior's discount for items they wanted to purchase.

"It's the high point of a lot of their days," she said.

"That's nice to hear, Maddie. And we all appreciate the coffee, especially me."

Muriel was the first to arrive, waddling in from the seniors' apartment a block away where she lived. She clutched a cake tin and plunked it on the table next to the coffee before she took her place. A lot of them brought snacks to class and I knew that for most this was an outing, a time to get together with friends.

"You're brave to walk on a day like this, threatening with rain," I told Muriel.

"My doctor says I should go for walks more. For the diabetes."

Marty and Dot were next. He grinned and saluted me. Dot placed a paper plate of lemon squares on the table next to the cake tin. She poured two cups of coffee, one for Marty and one for herself. You'd have to be blind not to see the look that passed between them. I swear I saw Marty blush as she handed him a foam cup.

"And how are you two lovebirds doing?" I asked.

Marty put a protective arm around Dot. "Oh, we're fine," he said.

"Couldn't be better," Dot added, and then blushing, she raised her left hand and her ring glimmered. Under the fluorescent light, the diamond looked big and sparkling.

"We're engaged," Marty whispered, a twinkle in his eye.

"Wow," I said. "Congratulations." And I meant it. Both of them deserved happiness. Maddie and Muriel came over to admire the ring. And as the others arrived, they, too, offered their congratulations before getting their coffee and squares. I thought that at any age, an engagement brings joy and happiness. It is a time of excitement.

Today there were six women and my one man, Marty. We were missing one of the women, and Phyllis told me that Gussie was under the weather and couldn't make it. "Gussie won't be able to see the ring until next time," someone said.

"That's okay," said Dot, beaming. "Marty and I will stop over there later and show her."

"Tell Gussie I hope she feels better," I said, laying pieces of purple ribbons across the table.

Eventually when they'd finished looking at Dot's ring, they sat down at the craft table. "I'm going to show you four ways to make a bow," I told them.

They dug out their scrapbook projects and I talked a bit about various ways to tie a bow, then went around and helped them individually. Muriel was quite adept at all of this, her sausage fingers handling the ribboning with ease, but Dot fumbled with her arthritic thumbs. I admired Marty patiently guiding her gnarled fingers to get a few awkward paper daffodils placed correctly. He wasn't working on his own project, but was helping Dot with hers.

Near the end of the hour, I got the picture of my parents out of my bag and when I had their attention I said, "I have a favor to ask all of you. I'm wondering if any of you know or recognize these people. They were killed in a car accident almost thirty years go." I held up the picture and let them pass it around. I saw a lot of head shakes. Marty looked down at the picture and shook his head, too.

When the picture got to Dot, she put on a pair of reading glasses, peered down at it and Dot elbowed Muriel. "Doesn't this look like that Sonya person? From a long time ago?"

"What Sonya person?" Muriel said.

Dot turned to me. "You said it was a car accident that killed them?"

I nodded.

She shook her head. "Not the right one then. Different thing. I have trouble remembering sometimes."

I put the picture back in the envelope and into my bag, but Muriel was still talking. "So much tragedy in the world," she said. "Makes you stop and think, don't it? Really makes you stop and think." And then the group of them began a discussion of all of the past catastrophes of Burlington, the deaths of people, a murder that had happened a long time ago, the disappearance and death of a college student and the ultimate discovery of her body, nothing about a car accident that had orphaned a three-year-old girl named Marylee. Dot was still puzzling over my picture.

"Dear," she said to Marty, "doesn't the girl look familiar to you?"

Marty glanced at the photo for less than half a second before he quickly said, "Never saw her before." His dismissal of it was so abrupt that I looked at him, but he was busy cutting a piece of fabric on the bias for the scrapbook Dot was making about her grandchildren.

"Marty," I asked tentatively. "I came across the name Danny Smythe and I was wondering if there was any relation to you."

His back stiffened. For several seconds he said nothing. Dot was eyeing him and the silence became uncomfortable.

"Marty?" she said. "Who is Danny Smythe? I've heard that name. Somehow it's familiar. Is this some long-lost relation of yours?"

"No," he said. "I don't know anyone by that name." His voice took on a strange edge when he spoke that didn't go unnoticed by Dot, or even me.

I wasn't prepared to let this go. I asked, "Danny Smythe isn't a relative of yours?"

" 'Fraid not." And he turned back to his fabric as he said it in a way that made me know that this discussion was over.

Midway through the morning, when we broke for refreshments, I ended up standing beside Dot. I said, "Is Marty okay? Is everything all right?"

She sighed. "That's just Marty. Don't mind him. He's had such heartache in his life."

"Really?" I thought of the feeling I'd had

at the craft fair, that I'd seen him before, that somehow, I knew him. I looked over at him now, as he poured himself another coffee.

Dot said quietly, "He went through a bit of a bad patch when he was younger. Such a sad story." She shook her head. "He was married once. His wife miscarried, somehow ended up blaming him for losing the baby. She ended up leaving him."

"Why would she blame him?" Marty was walking toward us smiling, two coffees in his hand.

"He doesn't like to talk about it, but after his wife left him, he never married again."

"Until now," I said.

"Until now," she said and grinned.

"What until now?" Marty grinned over her shoulder.

"Nothing, my sweet," she said.

I got myself another cup of coffee from the urn and then, because they were there, I grabbed a lemon square. I try not to eat sweets, but there it was. For the remainder of the class I helped the seniors with their individual projects, but I kept looking at Marty, at Dot. I was also thinking about the craft fair and what had triggered my reaction then.

At four-thirty it was time to pack up and

head back to Crafts and More. Marty and Dot lingered, talking to Maddie. While I was packing my bag, Marty approached me. "Dot reminded me of how abrupt and discourteous I was before. I want to apologize and tell you he's not worth it. He's just like his father."

I snapped my bag closed and stared at him. "What are you talking about? Who's not worth what?"

"Evan Baxter."

"What!"

"I think you deserve to know a bit about the family he comes from." Marty shook his head. "Dot and I were talking and we just don't want you to get hurt."

I continued to stare at him, mouth agape. Why on earth was he telling me this? Especially now when Evan appeared to be gone.

As if to answer my question, he went on. "I've seen you two together. I'm pretty perceptive for an old geezer." He tapped his head with his forefinger. "Actually, I saw you two in the coffee shop the other day. And I've been concerned for you since that time. That's why I was short with you earlier."

I still could not seem to find words.

Marty helped Dot on with her jacket and she said, "Marty's right. We don't want you to get hurt. You've had enough heartache in your life."

"I'm not going to get hurt." I'm not going to get hurt because my erstwhile almost boyfriend is no longer in my life, having totally disappeared, it seems, off the face of the earth. And why was Marty talking about this to me in the first place? And why should I answer?

"Dot?" He turned to her. "You knew the Baxter family better than I did."

"Not that much, Marty. Mostly it's just rumors."

"It was his sister, wasn't it?" Marty was still directing his comments to Dot.

"His sister, yes it was," she answered. "That's what I heard."

"Whose sister? Evan's?" I asked. What on earth were they talking about?

I felt like I'd been transported to some alternate universe and was eavesdropping on a conversation that had nothing to do with me. Yet it did. This was about Evan Baxter's sister. Was this important?

"What about her?" I demanded. Evan was visiting his sister — Mose had told me this.

Marty said, "She's in prison."

My eyes were wide. "Evan's sister is in prison?" No wonder Evan's eyes had gotten funny when I'd asked about his sister's quilts. "What for?" I found myself asking. My voice squeaked.

"It was for the fires, wasn't it, Dot? The fires?" Marty asked.

"Yes. Arson," Dot said.

"Evan's sister is in prison for *arson?*" I stared at them, dumbfounded.

Dot said, "I think it's unfair that she happened to be the one who got caught while all her little charges ran free."

Nothing was making any sense. I wish they'd speak English. "Marty," I said. "Can you quit talking to each other and explain this to me? What little charges?"

"A long time ago she set fires. Some had devastating results. She's older than Evan and the story is that she got Evan and some of the boys his age involved in setting fires in the community. Well, when they all were caught, the boys were underage and let go, while the sister was tried as an adult."

I was totally flabbergasted. "And this is all true?"

Both of them nodded.

"You said his whole family was dysfunctional," I prompted.

"His father," Marty said. "It was his father. His mother is now remarried and I think she's settled down."

"The whole family has," added Dot. "Except for the sister."

ELEVEN

I was in this kind of weird stupor when I got back to Crafts and More.

"What's the matter, Marylee? You look like you've seen a ghost."

"Not a ghost exactly. Well, just something weird. Really unsettling."

"Anything I can help with?"

I didn't want to share this, couldn't. "I'll get over it," I lied.

At the back, as usual, I checked my e-mail. Lots of spam, but nothing from Evan. Not that I expected anything.

He's visiting his sister. Mose had said that. Remembered snatches of conversation came to me: Evan saying that his sister "used to be" a quilter, and the look in his eyes when he'd spoken of her.

After the work day ended, I climbed the stairs to my apartment feeling weary. I didn't even think I wanted to work on my quilt or my mirror or even my counted cross-stitch. All I felt like doing was making a cup of tea, drawing myself a hot bubble bath and sitting in it with a nice little romance novel, complete with happy ending.

I'd found out nothing about the picture. No one had recognized it. Well, Muriel thought the woman reminded her of someone named Sonya, and then Marty had said he had no idea who Danny Smythe was, and then had gone on to tell me all these things about Evan. Evan, who still hadn't contacted me. I knew because I'd been checking my e-mail all day.

When I entered my apartment, I felt a cold breeze and stopped in my tracks. Ahead of me, the latch on my French door was pulled back and the door was open an inch. I drew in a breath, went to it. How had this opened up on its own? I had not left it open. I wouldn't have.

I opened the door farther and stepped out onto my rainy balcony. Something was wrong, and I stared at my porch for a moment. My rocking chair was not where I'd left it, not exactly. It had been moved slightly and sat facing the wall. Or maybe the wind had done this? I wondered if I should bring my chair inside. I decided to leave it for the time being. It was wet and

I'd wait until it dried off. Down below my balcony, my Saturn was safe and sound.

I went back inside, closed the door and pulled the little round bolt across. I checked it. It didn't seem especially loose. Nothing in my apartment looked disturbed. A twenty-dollar bill I'd left on the counter underneath a coffee mug was still there. Perhaps with the rain, the alley had become a wind tunnel, allowing the door to open. This had to be some weird fluke. Weird. Who was I kidding? Something strange was going on. Wind didn't explain the car alarm going off.

I let out a long sigh and sat down at my kitchen table. My telephone voice-mail light was flashing. Absently I hit the button, then sat straight up.

"Hey, Marylee, this is Evan. I'm sorry, sorry, *sorry,* I didn't call you sooner. Something came up. A kind of emergency here with my sister. I'm here now. I sent you about a dozen e-mails, but when you didn't answer, I thought I'd better check. I did, and it looks like none of them got through. At the place where she is, the Internet isn't always very reliable, so, I thought I'd do the old-fashioned thing and phone. But you're not home yet. I'll try later. Or you can call my cell." And he gave me the number.

The place where she is. The women's prison place where she was? And then I thought of something else — he'd been able to get through to Mose, but not to me? So the prison couldn't be too bad for sending e-mails.

I played back the message again, and then a third time. I closed my eyes and put my head on my kitchen table. When I raised my head, I realized that what I needed was a friendly face. I punched in Johanna's number and she answered on the first ring.

"I need a friend," I told her. "Are you busy? Can you come over? You would not believe what I found out about Evan."

"Evan? What? What did you find out? Hey, why don't you come here? Meredith and Ginger from church are here now. We're having a quick meeting about getting that book club going, but soon we're going to have supper. Meredith brought tons of food from the Greek restaurant where she works. And then the two of them have to leave for a church thingy."

"I could come later. Or not at all. I don't want to impose."

"You're not imposing at all. They both love you. We were just talking about you."

Twenty minutes later I found myself driving up Route 127 toward Johanna's place.

Meredith and Ginger were a bit flaky, but they were okay. A book club? That almost made me smile. Well, it might be nice to eat some Greek food and have some fun for a while.

I joined the group in Johanna's front room where a fire crackled and snapped in her stone fireplace. I don't know what Johanna had said about my situation, but Meredith's first comment to me was, "We hear you need some major cheering up. We've got plenty of food and ice cream for dessert."

"Great," I said.

"Have some Greek salad," Johanna said. Today my friend was wearing not only a red sock and a blue one, but one ear sported a small gold stud and the other a long dangly chandelier earring with tiny blue stones. I resisted the urge to ask her if she had another pair just like it.

On a coffee table in front of the fireplace were plates and bags of all kinds of Greek salad, gyros, falafel, all with generous doses of tzatziki sauce and feta cheese.

I filled my plate and we talked about favorite books and movies. I asked about their proposed book club and they invited me to join them. I responded that it sounded like fun.

The evening was light and casual, and was

just what I needed. At one point the three of them chatted and I found myself being drawn to the fireplace. I couldn't help it. I thought about the picture Evan had taken of the little girl beside the campfire. I looked away. I thought about his sister in prison for arson.

In a few minutes Ginger excused herself and went to the kitchen. She returned a moment later doing a bit of a dance and holding a container of Ben & Jerry's high above her head.

"Ice cream," she said. We dished it out into bowls until we'd killed the whole container.

"Did you know," Ginger said examining her spoon which held a rather hefty amount of the good stuff, "Burlington is the perfect city for jilted lovers."

"Oh really?" I said.

"Yes." Her face was thoughtful. "We are the city of teddy bears, right? And nothing makes a person feel better than a teddy bear. Plus —" she held her spoon high "— this is where Ben & Jerry's ice cream began. And what better way to drown one's sorrows than with ice cream?"

I ate spoonful after spoonful of the dessert, but it didn't do much to quell my nervousness or answer my questions.

After Meredith and Ginger left, Johanna and I sat quietly in front of the fire, drinking chamomile tea. She said, "Evan may or may not be a bum. I personally don't think he is. There's got to be some big misunderstanding, and I think we'll find out why he didn't call you. And did you go and see him like I told you to? You should —"

I interrupted her. "Evan did call. I wasn't there. He left a message. Also, I found out that Evan's sister is in a women's prison for arson. Evan was a part of her fire-setting gang."

"You want to run that by me again, slowly this time?"

I did.

"Evan's sister is in prison? I don't believe it. How could that be?" She combed her fingers through her hair. "Why didn't you tell me this sooner?"

"I didn't want to burden Meredith or Ginger with my big sob-story problems. Did you know he even had a sister? Did he ever talk about his sister to you?" I hugged a throw around me. The room was cooling down. Johanna picked up a log from the basket beside the fireplace and placed it on the embers.

"Once," she said. "On our second time out I remember him telling me he had to see his sister next week, but the way he said it I didn't press. I got this sort of strange feeling that it was a closed subject. Even for me, and you know how I press, Marylee."

"It's funny. I got that same feeling."

"Strange," she said, shaking her head.

"Apparently," I went on, "Evan and his sister come from a very dysfunctional home."

Johanna nudged a fireplace poker into the ashes until the fire blazed up. "I find that so hard to believe. I mean he goes to church and everything and he seems so nice." She pointed the poker at me. "But that could be part of it. As soon as he gets close to anyone, poof." She swept the poker around. "He's gone. First, his fiancée. Then me. Now you. You're right, Marylee, he has commitment issues. I mean, think about it this way, why would a guy be his age — what is he, thirty-two? — and not be married? This could be the reason, latent childhood issues. Maybe his dad? If his dad, like you said, wasn't that great a role model."

I moved away from her swinging fireplace poker. "Apparently he wasn't. Did you ever get to meet his parents?"

"Our relationship never progressed to that level." She put the poker back into the holder. "He did mention his father once."

"Really? What did he say?"

"Just that he was head of the church board or something. But maybe that's the guy his real mother remarried."

"Hmm." Evan didn't seem dysfunctional. He was so normal. At our meal together he seemed so natural, so genuine. I said, "And now to top everything off, I've got this new problem. I've got a balcony door that keeps unlocking itself."

"What do you mean?"

"What I mean is, I go over there and lock it and then the next day the bolt is pushed back again."

"Maybe it's just loose."

I hugged the blanket around me. "I'm thinking my house is haunted. My whole life is haunted. All I live with are ghosts."

She cocked her head at me. "That's very poetic, but not real. There's going to be a real explanation for it. Why don't you just get a new lock put in?"

For someone who taught English literature and dreamed about the right guy sweeping her off her feet, Johanna had a practical streak that was, at times, maddening. But maybe I needed to be brought back to reality.

Tomorrow I'd run down to the hardware store and get a new lock and install it. I'd get a true dead bolt this time, with a lock and key. I'd get the most expensive one. I wouldn't skimp on quality. If there's one thing I learned from my aunt, you don't skimp on quality when it comes to your own safety and security.

TWELVE

The following afternoon I found myself driving past Evan's shop on my way to drop off a bank deposit. It really wasn't on the way, and in fact I had to go out of my way to drive past his store, but I did it anyway.

Evan Baxter Photography was empty and I remembered the first time I'd stopped in, before I knew all there was to know about Evan. This time I didn't wander and look. This time I went straight to the counter and pressed the bell. No one came. The office door was opened slightly, but the darkroom door behind it was firmly closed.

I called out, "Mose? Evan?"

Nothing.

Maybe I should leave a note, I thought, rummaging in my purse for a pen and a piece of paper. I found a pen, but no paper. Maybe there was a scrap behind the counter somewhere, or something in the garbage can.

"I'm writing you a note!" I called out. "And then I'm leaving, but I'll be back, in case you're in the darkroom and can't come out."

Behind the counter and against the wall was a table stacked with paper and envelopes. On the top was a plain piece of white paper. I reached over, took the sheet and put it on the counter to write on. My heart stopped; I couldn't breathe. I turned back to the stack and there was the picture of my parents, the same one I'd given Evan, the same pose. But in this one, instead of standing on the shores of Lake Champlain, they were part of a studio shot. Behind them were dark studio drapes, and in one corner a tall vase of dried flowers. I picked up the photo and studied it. To me, it looked as if this were the real pose, the real picture, and the one I had was the phony, the composite, as Evan had told me. What was he doing with it? Why hadn't he told me he'd had this all along? What else was he lying to me about?

I drew in a breath. Is this why Evan had expressed surprise when he'd looked at the picture the first time? Was it because he'd had this one all along? The last time we were together, he'd practically begged me for my parents' picture so he could work on it some more. Why would he do that if he already had this one? What was going on?

I inserted the picture back in the stack of papers on the table, and without leaving a note, I walked out.

I was hurt. I felt betrayed. There was also this big part of me that was just plain mad. Upstairs after work, I got out my tool kit and my cordless drill to install the new dead bolt I'd bought that afternoon for my balcony doors. While I worked I listened to news on the radio and tried to convince myself that this old latch may have been the problem. It was too loose. It was too old. But I was fixing that. One by one, with steady determination, I could attack the problems in my life.

That job done, I decided I needed to get away from my apartment. It seemed oppressive, lonely. I dearly wanted to talk with Johanna. On Fridays she teaches a Writing Your Life Story class, so I was on my own. I need more friends, I thought to myself.

I grabbed my newest quilting magazine and headed down my back stairs. Half a dozen blocks later I found myself sitting in a booth in a little mom-and-pop eatery where a large woman in orthopedic shoes and a yellow apron with the name tag of

Faye told me that the special of the day was shepherd's pie plus coffee.

I ordered it.

She came back with my coffee, which smelled good, and said, "You the girl down at that knitting store, right?"

I smiled up at her. "Crafts and More. Yes, that would be me."

"Me, I'm not much of a knitter, but those two old biddies that ran it before you? They didn't have a lick of sense for business. I'm glad someone young and spunky has it now. Is it going good for you up there?"

"So far things are going fine. A lot of work, though. I hope I can make a go of it."

"Tell me about it. Christmas should find you pretty busy." Faye shifted the pen that was behind her ear to her pocket. "Lots of people shop downtown at Christmas because of all the gift shops and such like. That'll start happening in a month, so be ready for it."

"Thanks for the heads-up." I set my magazine on the table and stirred milk into my decaf.

"I heard you completely redid the inside. I'm not much of a knitter, like I said, but I've had a few customers tell me you got it all brightened up in there."

"I'm working on it. And I've got the business loan to prove it."

I'd kept some of the costs down by doing a lot of the renovations myself, all of the hammering and painting and decorating and sewing of curtains and installing new wainscoting. It was something I was supremely proud of; the only thing missing was Aunt Rose. I would love for her to see what I've been able to do on my own.

"Well," Faye said, patting my table. "I'll leave you to it. Your shepherd's pie will be up soon, and if you don't mind, can you tell me how you like the rolls? They're a new recipe I'm trying. Let me know what you think."

"Wait," I called after her. "Can I ask you something?"

"Sure, honey." She stood beside my table.

"Have you lived here a long time?"

"I was born here. Never even been away much. Why go anywhere when it's so pretty here?"

"I'm looking for some people. This would've been almost thirty years ago. Their names were Allen and Sandra Simson. Do those names ring a bell?"

She shook her head. "Sorry," she said, opening her palms in an I-don't-know gesture. "Never heard tell of them. You check the phone book?"

Of course I'd checked the phone book. And there were Simsons there, but I hadn't phoned them. I couldn't understand why. I could barely understand my own reaction, but every time I thought of phoning a random Simson, I'd hear my aunt's words: *"Don't go to Burlington. Evil in Burlington. Stay away from Burlington."* I had a photocopy of the picture with me so I dug it out of my bag and showed it to her. She squinted down at the fuzzy image.

"My dear, that's Sonya."

"Sonya?" This was the second time I'd heard the name Sonya. If this was someone named Sonya, why did I have her picture?

"Sonya who?"

"The last name escapes me. But the story was all over the news. They were killed. It was quite tragic." She shook her head. "Murdered. That's what the rumor said, but the police thought it was just an accident."

"The people I'm looking for were killed in a car accident."

She shook her head, gave me back the picture. "Wrong one then. And the sad thing was the woman who killed them got away. Those were the rumors, but nothing was ever solved, far as I know." She placed her hands on her hips. "Now she's a ghost. Haunts the place. Strange place Burlington is. We've seen our share of things. Ghosts and the like, too. Lots of ghosts here in Burlington. Old stories."

"I'll bet," I said, turning back to my coffee. Ghosts. It wasn't a ghost who'd opened up the door to my balcony or had gotten my car honking in the middle of the night. I didn't believe it was a ghost, and if it wasn't a ghost, did that mean there was real danger here? There could be real danger here. And my aunt had warned me about that very thing.

The day I'd graduated from high school I had come upon Aunt Rose crying in her bedroom. The following day I was to go away for the weekend with my best friend, Pammy, and her family to their cottage overlooking the ocean along the Oregon coast. Graduation was that afternoon and I'd come to ask Aunt Rose if she knew where my good jeans were. I was packing for the trip and needed to get my clothes ready.

I stood in the doorway, shifting from foot to foot. She was sitting on her bed and facing away from me, shoulders heaving. But I was young. Seventeen-year-olds have no patience for this. I went around and stood in front of her, hands on my hips until she noticed me. When she did, she patted the bed indicating that I should sit beside her. But the ceremonies were less than three hours away and I couldn't find my Calvin Klein jeans, and this was way more important to me than sitting with my aunt. So, I stood there sighing loudly, clearly annoyed. I was only graduating from high school. It wasn't as if I were moving to the end of the world. Why all the theatrics?

"Aunt Rose," I said. "I can't find my jeans."

Her eyes were red when she finally looked up at me. "Marylee," she began. "You need to promise me something. Tell me you'll promise me something."

I let out an exasperated sigh.

"I have to tell you this, Marylee. I need to tell you something very, very important. And you need to listen and you need to promise me something."

I could tell that there would be no jeans information forthcoming until I made a promise, or at least said I would listen.

"Okay," I said finally. I didn't roll my eyes, but in my heart my eyes were rolling. "What is it?"

"Promise me this, Marylee. That you will never, ever go back to Burlington, Vermont. That you will not."

"Why?" I said. "Why shouldn't I?"

Up until this point all suggestions by me that we travel there on vacation had been met by shrugs and "It's too far" and "There's nothing for us there."

"Don't I have family there?" I would sometimes ask.

"Not anymore," she'd always retort.

But now her eyes were wide, fearful and her shoulders were shaking. And I realized that her shoulders had not been heaving because of tears, but from fear.

I'd never made that promise.

My shepherd's pie arrived. It tasted as good as it smelled and I was glad I'd gone out for supper instead of shoving a chicken-meatball dinner in the microwave. I should do this more often, I thought. Go out for a nice home-cooked meal. I may be good with a hammer and nails and needle and thread and itsy pieces of glass, but I was not a great cook. My culinary efforts stopped at home-made pizza. As I took a mouthful of the excellent casserole, I thought again of my aunt.

For a grad gift she'd given me the wooden quilting frame that now sits in my living room with a card I have kept. Since her death I have read and reread it so many times, I know the inscription by heart:

There are so many things, Marylee, that I wish I could have been for you. I wish I could have been mother and father. I've watched you grow into the wonderful and beautiful young woman you are today. Your mother and father would have been so proud of you. In fact, I think they ARE proud of you. Have a wonderful life in Oregon. Never leave its shores.

Even in her graduation card there was that warning. Whatever you do, stay in Oregon. Stay home. There's no need to travel.

The day after graduation, Pammy and I and three other girls from my high school had spent a weekend at Pammy's cottage. Thoughts of danger in Vermont had been far from my mind as the four of us had traipsed around the shoreline talking, laughing, sharing stories from the past and dreams for the future. Pammy and I would be going to the same college in the fall, the place where in my final year I would meet Mark. Pammy was to be my maid of honor. Funny how things can change so in a matter of months.

When I finished my meal, I told Faye the rolls were delectable. I left a generous tip and chatted for a few more minutes. I invited her to my store. "It's more than a knitting store now," I said with a grin. "I've got a whole section of gift items. Be sure to tell your customers that."

"I will."

"And I'll tell my customers if they want really, really good meals to come here." I took one of her cards and a takeout menu and shoved them into my pocket.

When I got back to my apartment nothing had changed. I did a few hand stitches on my quilt but couldn't focus. Was I safe here? Despite the new bolt, I felt uneasy.

I still felt lonely and so I looked up a number in my PDA and called Portland. When I moved out here, Pammy and I had vowed to keep in touch via e-mail. We have, but not a lot. Life gets in the way sometimes.

"Hello."

"Pammy? It's me, Marylee."

"Marylee! It's so nice to hear from you. We were just talking about you."

"You were?"

"At Bible study. How's the yarn shop going?"

"It's great. It's going well. It's nice out here."

"That's wonderful! Everyone out here still misses you. When're you coming home?"

Home. I blinked. "I don't know. I'm pretty busy here. The store keeps me hopping."

"How about sending some pictures?"

"I will. I will. That's a good idea. Um . . . how is . . . ?"

"He-who-shall-not-be-named?"

"Yeah."

"They're married now. They're in our Bible study. She's actually quite nice. I think they're expecting a baby. Someone told me that."

I gripped the phone.

"But he's still King Jerk, so you're not missing anything."

"Good, then."

"You happy there? Things are going well?"

I thought of the man who'd leaned against the bus shelter and looked up at me, and said, "Everything's fine."

We chatted a few more minutes, but clearly we were running out of things to talk about and when we said our goodbyes I realized just how much I had moved on, just how different my life now was.

I was back to my quilting frame when my cell phone rang. I rummaged through my bag for it. And nearly dropped it when I saw where the call was originating from. Evan Baxter Photography! I thought about not answering it at all. But on the third ring I did. I needed to know things. I had questions for him. I needed to know what he'd been doing all along with that picture of my parents.

"Marylee?" He sounded far away, distant. "Marylee? Is that you?"

"Yes."

"I'm so sorry. I've tried reaching you for three days. I was called away. Rather suddenly."

"So you said."

"Remember I told you about my sister?"

"Yes."

"Sometimes I have to come and take care of her. It's two hundred miles from Burlington."

"Oh." Where was the nearest women's prison? I had not a clue. Montpelier?

"Wow! I can't believe I finally got a hold of you. This is crazy. I'm so sorry."

"It's okay."

"You sound sort of funny. Are you okay?"

"I'm okay."

"I'm calling with a question."

"Okay."

"Does the name Adam Samuels mean anything to you?"

"Samuels." Something about the name made me blink, stop, catch my breath. Why?

"Just wondering," he said. "I saw that name written along the margin of two of the pages in the accounts book. I was just wondering if you'd heard that name before."

"Adam Samuels." I said the name aloud. No, it wasn't familiar in any real sense, yet why did the saying of this name make me suddenly think of mirrors? "I'm not sure. No, I haven't heard that name before." And I hadn't. It was more a sense of it than any overt knowledge as to who that was.

"I'll do some more digging, see what I can come up with."

"Okay."

"And I'm calling for another reason. I'm wondering, hoping that you'll be my guest at that gallery showing I was telling you about."

"What?"

He cleared his throat. He seemed a bit nervous and said, "I would be honored if you'd accompany me. I know it's short notice. It's Sunday. Like in two days Sunday, but like I said, I've been trying to get a hold of you."

How could I say yes when I knew he might eventually hurt me? How could I say yes when there were so many unanswered questions about him? He'd had a picture of my parents all along. He came from a dysfunctional family and his sister was in prison. There was no way I could say yes!

"Yes," I said. "I'd love to." As soon as I

said it I wondered at my sanity.

"I'm so sorry I didn't get to you sooner. I left without my phone charger and then things got really hectic here. I'm sorry. I'll call tomorrow. But I'm glad you've agreed to go with me."

Who was I kidding? I had said yes because I simply wanted to. I wanted to see him. I wanted to be with him.

THIRTEEN

All night long I tossed and turned. I woke thinking I'd dreamed about mirrors, but I couldn't remember the specifics. Several times I got up and looked out of my front window. The smoking man wasn't there. I checked my clock and that the French doors to my balcony remained shut and locked. All night long I kept trying the name Adam Samuels on my tongue. I did an Internet search. There were about a gazillion Adam Samuelses, and even when coupled with Burlington it yielded too many hits to be useful. And since I didn't know what I was looking for, I gave that up.

In the morning in my shop after getting my coffee — Evan wasn't there — I wrote the name Adam Samuels on a piece of paper and looked at it. Saying it out loud made me think of mirrors, but it wasn't a scared feeling; I didn't feel afraid when I said the name. No, that wasn't it. It was something else. I didn't know what.

The entry bell jangled and I made my way to the front of the store to help a trio of women buy craft fabric and yarn.

"Do you have jewelry-making supplies?" one of them asked. "I'd like to get into making my own jewelry."

"Sorry," I told her. "I wish I had room for every craft but I just don't." Then I told them where in town they might find these items. But the whole time I waited on them and chatted cheerfully about the weather, which was becoming cooler, I was trying on the name Adam Samuels.

Right after lunch, the back door opened and Barbara came in with the cold. She shivered affectedly as she hung up her fluffy faux-fur coat on a hanger. "Getting cold out these days. How's the morning been?"

"Can I ask you a question?"

"Shoot."

"Does the name Adam Samuels ring any bells?"

She cocked her head. "Not really. What's this in connection with?"

"I don't know. I'm not sure. And, in answer to your question, it's not been too busy. I've had time to dust and clean a bit."

"Well, how about this?" she said. "Why don't you take the rest of the afternoon off, then, Marylee. I can handle the afternoon if you want to go shopping or anything. You spend too much time here. But, I've told you that before."

I thought about that. "Perhaps that's a good idea. I'd planned to go through the inventory a bit, and maybe try to figure out that new computer program, but the afternoon off? Hmm."

I knew exactly what I would do with an afternoon to myself.

Half an hour later I was sitting at the microfilm machine in the library, looking through *Burlington Free Press* articles from 1982. It was a long shot, but if the name Adam Samuels was printed in the ledger book, maybe looking for news articles from that time period might come up with something. As I moved through the microfilm, I listened to the quietness of this old library. The only sound was the whoosh of the machine as I moved through the stories.

I worked slowly, slowly looking for any reference to Adam Samuels. I found nothing. I shifted on my seat. I had pushed my chair back to leave when I saw it. A huge headline — how could I have missed it? *Hardware Store Torched. Police have confirmed that arson destroyed Samuels Hardware, killing owners Adam and Sonya Sam-*

uels. Several bushfires have been set recently, and the police feel this might be the work of the same person or persons.

I continued to read. The fire had spread quickly, burning the hardware store to the ground. Firefighters had arrived on the scene in time to save the neighboring buildings. I continued flipping forward and backward through the articles. Nearby someone coughed, but in a few minutes I had my answer. And it was one that shocked me to the core of who I was. The obituary read that Adam and Sonya Samuels were survived by their three-year-old daughter, Marybelle, Sonya's sister, Rose West, and various other brothers and sisters.

I read those lines three times. I had turned to stone in my chair. *Was this . . . Was this . . . Could this be me?*

But no, of course not. Aunt Rose had always said "car accident." Or had she? I leaned my head into my hands and tried to remember. When I had asked about the "car accident," why hadn't she corrected me? Or was this story I found a total coincidence? Yet, how many accidents would kill parents and leave a three-year-old child an orphan in the same year in Burlington with the same name? And an aunt Rose.

I wondered, had my aunt merely read

about this and then decided to "use" this convenient accident to explain who I was? But then why not say it was a fire right from the beginning? I never dreamed of hardware stores and fires. Why did I dream about mirrors and not fires?

I read more. Witnesses reported seeing a woman fleeing the scene, and I remembered what Faye from the restaurant had said about someone named Sonya. She'd said the rumors said murder. Several witnesses wondered if this was the work of a gang of young boys who set fires to fields in the area.

And then another thought, a more sinister thought, a thought that made me choke. Evan had been with a gang of boys who'd set fires. His sister was in jail for arson. I calculated. Evan would have been around seven? Eight? No! I could not bend my mind around this fact. I quickly scanned through the rest of the stories. The police had never found the people responsible for the blaze. Someone named Daniel Smythe had been brought in for questioning and let go. That name! The person Evan thought was stealing money from the store, which I now knew, maybe, to belong to Adam and Sonya Samuels, who were my parents.

I left the microfilm machines and sidled over to the computer. Now that I knew what

I was looking for, I quickly found more articles when I searched for Adam and Sonya Samuels with *hardware store* and *fire.* I was able to read online accounts of the fire, but basically learned nothing new. There was very little about the three-year-old girl who'd "gone to live with relatives."

I scanned backward and forwards for mentions of Evan or his sister, but then realized that if they had been children, their names would have been kept out of the paper.

I read the obituary again and learned that Adam had one brother, Warren. Warren Samuels and his wife, Gabby, and Adam's parents had been alive at the time of the accident and living in Burlington. There were others as well. I carefully wrote down all of the names, and the address in Burlington where Adam and Sonya Samuels had lived.

A thin, lanky girl with black jewelry came in and asked how much longer I would be. She had a school project, she explained. I wanted to scream at her, *You have a school project? This is my life!* But I didn't. "I'll just be a minute," I said quietly. "I'm almost finished here."

I was shaking by the time I left the library and climbed into my car. I should have been congratulating myself. I was, after all, "getting somewhere." Yet I couldn't move.

After making several false starts, getting hung up at road construction, and getting turned around again, I found the street where the Samuelses had lived. The good thing about my ex-fiancé, the only good thing, was that he'd had one of those little car GPS units. You just plug in the address and a soft female voice guides you to your destination. That would have served me well now, I thought as I became increasingly turned around on Burlington side roads.

The address ended up being a street full of majestic houses and old weepy-looking trees. Some of the homes along this street were quite well maintained with groomed gardens even at this time of year when brown seemed to be the predominant color. The house I was looking for, the house I eventually found, was a wooden Cape Cod with gables and a wraparound front porch on a corner lot. It looked as if it used to be a pale peach, but it was faded and paint had flaked in places.

The cement walk that ran from the porch to the sidewalk was heaving in places and leggy weeds grew up through the cracks. I wondered why the house didn't generate more feelings of familiarity within me. A

For Sale sign hung forlornly near the walkway. There was one large-trunked leafless tree square in the middle of the front yard. I looked and looked and tried to remember. Maybe I had this all wrong. Maybe I wasn't Marybelle Samuels. Maybe my parents had died in a car accident or maybe Rose had made up the whole thing and I was now on a wild-goose chase.

Dirty plastic children's toys were piled on the front porch. They looked as if they'd been dragged through the dirt and then discarded or maybe just played with hard. The whole place had a cast-off look about it, windswept and a bit grimy. Or maybe it only looked that way because this was the beginning of winter, and all the houses on the street looked this way. Or maybe it was because I felt this way.

The windows of the house were covered by filmy, lacy curtains of the kind that elderly ladies favor. A curtain moved slightly, as if someone had been looking out at me, and I felt like a weird kind of stalker. I put my Saturn in gear and drove slowly forward. It was quiet on the street, no traffic, so driving at ten miles per hour was an option.

At the end of the property was a shed, a small copse of trees and a sandbox with more children's toys. I drove past slowly and a feeling of dread settled in my stomach and caused me to clutch at my belt. Was I going to be sick? In my mind I saw mirrors. In my mind, mirrors were chasing me. I considered all of this as I pulled onto the highway and drove back to my shop. It was an ordinary outbuilding, a very small shed, hardly big enough to hold a lawn mower and a few bicycles. Why had it engendered such a feeling of fear?

The closer I got to Crafts and More, the more I began to wonder if the whole thing was something I'd merely imagined, another event in a line of strange coincidences since I'd come back here.

I called Barbara on my cell and asked her for Dot's address. She looked it up and gave it to me. I decided to go there, not call, but go there in person.

I drove down a winding road to the town house where Dot lived. And as I drove toward it, I have to admit I began to feel a bit guilty about the fact that I was leaving Barbara in the shop, although, it was not very busy today, and this wouldn't take long. And this was important.

I finally found the town house, and as I rang the bell for number fifty-two, I hoped Dot would be there, and Marty wouldn't.

When Dot saw it was me standing on her front porch, she beamed. "Well, to what do I owe this pleasure?"

"I have a couple of questions, Dot. Can I come in?"

"Well, of course, Marylee. Would you like some tea? Coffee? A cold drink?"

"That's okay, I can't stay too long." Then I thought better of it. If I stayed a while maybe she would talk more. "On second thought, maybe tea would be nice."

Dot's town house was all on one level with a garage. It was nicely done and I was immediately surprised at the bright colors. Hardwood floors and a hot-pink area rug. And clear glass furniture. On the coffee table nicely framed in white was a picture of Marty and Dot. They looked like a happy, cozy couple. I followed her into her kitchen and she filled the kettle with water and plugged it in. "You must be very happy," I said.

"I am. I've been a widow for a long, long time. It's so nice to have Marty. We are so suited to each other."

She dropped a few tea bags into a flowered pot. "I came because you recognized the woman in the picture I had as Sonya. Would that be Sonya Samuels?"

She stopped, looked at me. "Yes, I believe

so. Yes. That was her name."

"Did you know her?"

She shook her head. "I knew *of* her, as the saying goes." She poured boiling water in the teapot.

"In class you said that there was some bad business early on with Marty. Did that have anything to do with Danny Smythe? Do you know who Danny Smythe is?"

She bent her head and regarded me. "I really have not heard that name."

"Danny Smythe worked in the Samuelses' store." I wasn't totally sure of this, but I said it anyway.

"Well, that I don't know." She placed a teacup in front of me, and we sat on stools at her kitchen counter to drink it.

I said, "I think Marty knows who he is. And is, ah, maybe protecting him. And you're sure you don't know the name? Even from a long time ago?"

She shook her head. "I've lived here a long time. My first husband, he worked on the ferry before he died too young. His heart."

"I'm sorry to hear that."

But before I could stop her, she launched into a story of Burlington in the early days. I kept surreptitiously looking at my watch and thinking about Barbara at the store all by herself.

"So, the name Danny Smythe is no one that I know."

"I'm wondering if you could do something for me?" I hesitated to ask her, but I was really desperate. "Could you maybe see if you could find out from Marty who Danny is? Can you ask him again? Maybe he's forgotten."

"Well, I could try, dear, but I don't believe this is anyone Marty knows or is related to. Marty is a very honest and upright person. Lately, though, all the wedding preparations have been a little much for him. So, if he seems distracted if you ask him questions, well, have patience. And if I could be so bold, you've seemed a bit distracted lately, too, dear."

"Maybe." Maybe I've got a good reason to feel distracted, I thought.

Later, back at my shop, I got out the Burlington phone book and looked up Samuels. There were a couple of columns of them. I saw a few W. Samuels and one G. Samuels, plus their addresses. Do I just phone them willy-nilly or do I have a plan? Okay, a plan. I'll start at the top of the list and ask if they know Adam and Sonya Samuels or if they are related to them. And then depending on the reaction I get, I'll introduce myself. I'll continue down the list until

I find someone who knew them, and knew me. I had almost finished punching in the number for the first Samuels when I remembered that it was arson that had killed my parents. It was why I hadn't called any Simson sooner. And now I knew even more. What if a family member had done this? What if it was another Samuels from whom my aunt was running? I stopped in mid-dial and put the phone back in its cradle. There had to be another way to find out what I needed to know.

Fourteen

I stood in front of my full-length mirror and groaned. Right now I had on an ankle-length black pencil skirt slit up to mid-thigh. As I turned this way and that I decided that to wear a skirt this formfitting I would need to lose five pounds.

My deep purple blouse wasn't working either. The neckline was too low. I'd be self-conscious all night and would be constantly tugging at it, pulling it up. I held my hair off my face when Johanna stood at the foot of my bed holding yet another outfit for me to try on. "You are one hot mama in that," she said.

I let my hair drop. "Hot mama is not the look I'm going for." I pulled off the blouse. "And the skirt's too long, and the slit's too high. I don't know if this is a formal occasion or not. Maybe I should just wear jeans and a sweater. Maybe it's a casual thing."

"Evan didn't tell you?"

"He's wearing a suit, but he's the reason for the show."

"Men!" Johanna exclaimed, holding up a plain black dress so I could see it. Johanna and I were in my apartment and my bed was covered with discarded clothes. So far I'd tried on a pink sheath dress, a brown pantsuit, wide plaid gaucho pants and a variety of tops and jewelry and scarves and shoes.

Johanna wanted to help me choose the perfect outfit. Trouble was, my heart just wasn't in all of this. All I wanted to do was to curl up in a ball and forget about the fact that I had to go out with Evan. I couldn't forget what I'd learned, that people had seen a woman fleeing the scene of the fire that had killed my parents, and that Evan's older sister was in prison for arson and that my name really wasn't Marylee. I was Marybelle. Trouble was, I liked the name Marylee. I've grown into the name through the years. It suits me. It's the name of a person who makes quilts and does counted cross-stitch in her spare time the same way other people do Sudokus. Marybelle? While I tried on clothes, I tried on the name, Marybelle Samuels, but it felt as discarded as the bed full of clothes that I'd tried on and cast off.

Johanna held a black dress up for me to see. "This might work. If it fits."

"If it fits. Your sister's probably skinnier than me, if she's anything like you."

She shook her head. "No, you try that one on. If that one fits, it would be perfect. My sister said that this one can either be dressed up or dressed down, depending."

I held the dress against the front of me and said, "How do I look as a Marybelle?"

"Promise me you won't change your name to Marybelle, or I will be forced to not be your friend anymore."

I know she was just trying to make me feel better, adding a bit of humor to a very strange situation.

"Not in this lifetime," I said. By now I had the black dress on and it fit as if it had been sculpted exactly for me. It swept softly to my knees and was not too tight in the places it shouldn't be too tight and not too loose in the places it shouldn't be too loose.

"You still look like a hot mama," Johanna said. "Evan will flip."

"Oh, dear, too much?"

She shook her head. "No, that one is perfect. That's the dress for the gallery. Now, how about some jewelry?" And she held up a huge and gaudy piece of costume jewelry from my aunt's stash.

"Eww, no," I said.

"But it's perfect."

"No, Johanna. First of all, it's not me and second, I can't believe I'm taking fashion advice from someone who wears two different colored socks and a different earring in each ear."

"I do that on purpose," she said defensively.

I settled on a pearl necklace that was my aunt's and dangly silver earrings, and refused Johanna's helpful offer to put highlights in my hair then and there. I would wear my hair loose and straight with a silver barrette holding it back on one side. I twirled in front of the mirror in the dress. "You sure your sister won't mind? This dress looks expensive."

"My sister won't mind. You'd love my sister."

Johanna also ended up loaning me a short black jacket with a fur collar, a sparkly little purse, her own jeweled barrette, soft leather gloves and a cashmere scarf in a deep shade of peach.

I pulled off the dress, groaned and flopped back on my bed in my slip. "What am I thinking? I can't go out with him. I've had so many upsets these past couple of weeks. I just don't think I'm up to this. Not with all the stuff I know now. How can I go and pretend that everything's just hunky-dory? And we're having an ordinary little date?"

"Marylee, Marylee, Marylee, you are up to it. You're getting so close to figuring everything out. You thought that that picture wasn't your parents? And now you know it is. Your mother *was* that beautiful woman in the picture and you know her name. Plus, plus, there's a busload of Samuelses in the phone book. Three busloads. You've got lots of relatives. Probably."

"But Evan? What if he . . . ?" I couldn't say it. I could just barely think it.

"What if he set the fire that killed your parents?"

I nodded.

"Personally," she said, "I think that's highly unlikely. For a little kid to light a fire that does that much damage? That only happens in horror movies. Think about it — a ten-year-old kid, for example, just wouldn't have the knowledge or the ability to commit an arson of this magnitude and then elude the cops for all these years."

I wanted to believe her, but wasn't sure. Because what if it was his sister, his psychopathic sister who'd set it and then involved Evan and his friends somehow? "But he recognized my parents when he saw the picture the first time. I know he did. And well, if he didn't do the deed, I have a strong feeling he knew who did. Maybe he was even there, the arsonist's apprentice."

Johanna laughed. "Now that *does* sound like the name of a horror movie! Marylee, just go and have a good time. Because when you think about it, why would he ask you if you knew the name Adam Samuels when he already knew?"

"Maybe to gauge my reaction? Who knows? And it's not a date, Johanna. It's a fact-finding mission."

"You keep telling yourself that."

I tried on the whole ensemble again and looked at myself in the mirror. This would do.

The gallery reception was from five until eight the following evening, and then Evan and I and the owner of the gallery and a few other select people were going out for dinner. I hated to admit it, but I was looking forward to being with Evan. I would need to continually remind myself throughout the evening of my serious purpose.

Some things just aren't meant to be, I suppose, and the gallery opening was one of those things. Or maybe I'd been looking forward to it too much, expected too much.

If I'd had any doubts about Evan being the arsonist's apprentice before the evening began, I had none by the end of it.

The evening started nicely enough. At four forty-five Evan rang the buzzer at my back door. I opened the door and stepped out.

"You look . . ." He paused and I could feel his gaze. "You look beautiful."

"You look pretty nice yourself," I retorted. "A tux. Wow!" He looked way more than pretty nice. A man in a tux always looks way more than pretty nice.

He took my arm and led me to the passenger side of his car. "The tux was my mother's idea," he told me. "She said that a tux was warranted for an occasion such as this." I caught a whiff of his musky aftershave and my heart did a little flip. Fact-finding mission, fact-finding mission, fact-finding mission.

"Will your parents be there?" I slid into the seat, trying not to look at him too hard.

"They will, and they're anxious to meet you."

"Your sister? Will she be there, too?"

He looked away from me as he shut the door. "Afraid not."

This was the first time I'd been in his car, a cute little silver Honda SUV. "Nice car," I said when he drove it out of the alley.

"I need a car like this," he explained, "to haul all my camera gear everywhere. It's practical."

The inside of it was immaculate. I could even see little vacuum marks in the upholstery and I wondered if he'd cleaned it especially for this night out. We were listening to classic rock and when I said I liked the music, he said it was satellite radio. "I'm on the road a lot," he said. "And I enjoy my music."

I liked his choice of radio stations. Too many guys try to impress their dates with choices like classical music that they would never dream of listening to at home.

"I'm looking forward to this," I said as we headed up Main Street.

"I hope you enjoy it." He braked at a light and looked over at me. "Even though they're part of the job, I never like these sorts of things." And then his eyes flitted forward. "I'm glad you're with me."

"Do you get nervous at events like this?" I asked.

He tapped his fingers on the steering wheel. "Not as much as not liking to have to act a certain way." Whatever he had overcome in his early years, his face didn't show it. Tonight he looked like a little boy on his way to a party.

I was not here to have fun. I was not here to admire this handsome man in a tuxedo. I was not here to marvel at his photographs. A whole lot of events had transpired and a whole lot of facts had been unearthed since our memorable afternoon, and I needed answers.

As I sat next to him, I kept thinking that what I should be feeling was fear, not this giddy attraction to a handsome man. Why wasn't I more afraid? But then something else reminded me that my feelings weren't the greatest things to trust. I didn't have the best track record for trusting feelings.

We rode in silence for a few minutes. I wondered if I should start my fact-finding mission now or wait until we got there. Wait until we get there, I decided. Keep the talk small for now.

We chatted about inconsequential things until Evan pulled into the small parking space next to the gallery. I had never been to the NeWorks Gallery. It was on a street full of similar small galleries and fine-arts and gift stores and private museums in South Burlington.

NeWorks Gallery was a small space with hardwood floors and barn board walls. I liked it immediately. I'd been toying with the idea of replacing the old linoleum floors of my shop with wood. That was on my list of things to do as soon as I made a bit more money. But unlike a new hardwood floor, this floor with its dark knots and murky swirls looked as if it had been here for centuries. Evan's photos were artfully displayed on the wood walls, each with its own spotlight. There were also a number of wooden art easels that displayed some of his larger works, including the picture of the girl beside the campfire. Discreet little spotlights highlighted these photos as well.

In the center of the room, three tables were covered with floor-length white cloths. One held a punch bowl, bottles of wine and assorted stemware. Another was spread with crystal plates containing oysters, shrimps, mountains of cheese, and what looked as though it could possibly be caviar. These were intermingled with baskets of crackers and baguettes. The third table contained silver platters of small sweet squares. In the back by the wall was a microphone on a stand.

We hung our coats in a cloakroom at the rear. At the far end of the cloakroom were the restrooms. I made a note of that. Across from the cloakroom was a closed door, which I assumed led into an office of some kind.

A tall and thin to the point of cadaverous middle-aged woman with a multitude of bangle bracelets and layers of necklaces shook my hand, introduced herself as Leila, and told me how delighted she was to meet me. But when Evan mentioned that I owned and ran Crafts and More, her eyes seemed to look past me and she said, "Oh, the old Knitting Barn?"

I said, "It's called Crafts and More now, and we sell a lot more than yarn."

Evan said proudly, "Marylee is an artisan in her own right. Soon it's her you'll be displaying here, her crafts. She makes mirrors. And paper."

"That's nice." Leila put a much bejeweled hand on Evan's arm and looked away from me. "Evan, we need to go over a few of the details for tonight. The guests will begin to arrive momentarily, and then people will mill, mill, mill and eat, eat, eat and drink, drink, drink and hopefully buy, buy, buy." Her hands with their long red nails flitted in the air while she chanted this. "I've gotten a good quantity of brochures made up. There's also plenty of food. About an hour into the program, we'll begin the formal part of the evening. I'm absolutely livid —"

she looked around her "— that the live music isn't here yet. They should have been set up at least half an hour ago."

Every time she moved, she jangled. She wore wide black shiny pants and a long silk shirt that looked faintly Asian. All along the bottom edge of it were beads that clattered against each other whenever she shifted her position. Or were they shells? Without bending down and grabbing the hem, I couldn't tell.

A few minutes later two musicians arrived and unpacked their instruments out of two large cases; an upright bass and a cello. Visitors began arriving, singly and in groups, and their attire ranged from formal to jeans.

A moment later Leila left us and talked with a thin woman, pretty, with straight hair to her waist.

Evan leaned into me and said, "The fun begins. Can I get you a drink?"

"Punch," I said, smiling up at him.

By now people were beginning to balance tall-stemmed glasses of wine and plates of cheese and crackers while they walked around looking at the pictures. When Evan returned with a crystal cup of punch, I said, "So, you have to speak at this, too?"

He groaned. "Don't remind me." He patted his breast pocket. "I've got it all written out on three pieces of paper. I'm not a great public speaker."

"You'll do just fine."

The musicians in the corner had started up. It was oddly minor and tuneless, and I wasn't sure I liked it. The punch was good, though, quite citrusy and tangy.

More and more people began filling the small space. It was getting warm and close. Although he tried to stay near me, Evan was constantly being strong-armed by fellow artists or fans. I spoke with a wife of a photographer who praised Evan's work. I spent a few minutes with a person in blue jeans who'd walked in off the street. The party was not a private one. Leila didn't care who bought pictures, it seemed.

In the corner, Evan was talking with three women — the one with the waist-length hair and two others. They were joined by a very large man with a handlebar mustache. Evan saw me, waved me over, but on my way over to the group, I was accosted by a paunchy middle-aged man who asked me whether I thought Evan's photos were representational, emotional or realistic. I smiled sweetly and said all three.

When I looked up for Evan again, the little group had dispersed, so I decided to walk the perimeter by myself. There was a circular grouping of black-and-white faces on one wall. I stood back and looked at them.

On another wall were children, lots of them. I was close to the front door now and saw Mose smoking outside and leaning against the building. If Evan found these kinds of gatherings difficult, Mose looked as if he hated them. I wondered why he'd come at all. I became conscious that he was looking at me as I was looking at him. I quickly looked away and moved toward the table.

I picked up a brochure. On the front of the three-fold glossy pamphlet was the girl in the faded pink sneakers pointing at the fire. I found the original on one of the wooden display frames and went over to it. I studied again the girl in the ratty shoes, one hand in her pocket, the other one pointing at the flames with her forefinger, fire reflected in her grave eyes.

I looked at it for a long time. *I find the colors of fire so fascinating.* Evan had said this. Something in the picture chilled me. I looked at her eyes. I could not take my eyes off the flames. It was as if the girl herself, instead of merely pointing at the fire, had cast the fire into existence by pointing. I felt suddenly ill and I wrapped my arms around me. Who was this girl? I'd seen several pictures of her on the wall of children. The chatter in the gallery seemed to fade around me as I stared at the one somber girl pointing at flames. *I find the colors of fire so fascinating.* I backed away from the picture and right into the arms of Evan Baxter.

"Hey," he said, touching my shoulder. "I saw you standing all by yourself over here. So sorry to have left you alone. I brought over my parents for you to meet."

"Oh . . . um . . ." My throat was dry. I looked up into his eyes. Was I looking into the face of a monster?

"Mom, Dad, this is Marylee. Marylee, these are my parents, Louise and Todd."

A moment later I found myself shaking hands with a very normal looking middle-aged couple. Evan's father looked as if he were dressed for an uncomfortable Sunday service with a suit and tie and stiff shirt. His mother wore a one-piece dress in gray wool accented with a red scarf.

"It's so nice to meet you, Marylee," said Evan's mother, leaning forward to shake my hand. "Evan's told us so much about you."

Marty had told me that Evan's mother had remarried after a bad marriage. Evan didn't look like his mother, but he was the same size as the man who introduced himself as Evan's father, and maybe they had the same nose. But a lot of people have noses like that.

"You must be very proud of your son." I put a slight emphasis on the word *son.* "These are beautiful photos."

"We are proud of him."

"That one," I said of the girl and the fire. "That one is especially striking."

"Oh, that. That's our sweet Daphne," Louise said.

"Daphne?" From where I stood I could see the girl's haunted eyes. This was no ordinary child.

"My niece," Evan said. "My sister's daughter."

"She lives with us most of the time now," Louise said.

"Oh?" I said. But they didn't answer me.

Leila was bending into the microphone. "Hello? Hello?" The microphone squealed. She tapped it. "Can you all hear me on this?"

When she had our attention, she said, "Good evening, ladies and gentlemen. On behalf of the NeWorks Gallery, I want to thank you for coming out this evening of the showing of this wonderful new artist, Evan Baxter. We at NeWorks pride ourselves in discovering new talent and new artists. Evan is one of Burlington's best new photographers." She extended her arm in the direction of where Evan used to be, beside me. He wasn't there. There was a moment of narrowing her eyes as Leila scanned the room for him. I looked around me, too. He'd just been here. Louise and Todd were here, but no Evan.

Applause. I clapped along with the group, many of whom found it a challenge to clap while holding their wine and plates of food.

". . . In a few moments I'm going to call Evan up and say a few words . . ."

I looked around me. Evan had truly disappeared.

"But before he comes up here, I want to give you a brief intro into our night's guest of honor, a little bit about his childhood and where his love for the photographic arts was really born . . ."

I would listen to this. This might tell me something.

Then I smelled something, or thought I did. Smoke? Had someone lit a chimney somewhere? I looked around me. No one else seemed to be noticing this. I looked to the front door where Mose had stood casually leaning there smoking just moments ago. He was not there. And then suddenly it hit me. It was Mose who'd stood leaning against the bus shelter at night looking up at my apartment. I recognized him and gasped.

But why? I listened to Leila go on about Evan's humble and wonderful beginnings in Burlington, how photography was something Evan had always been interested in, even as a boy . . . while I thought about Mose and Evan. And how they were both gone now and I smelled smoke.

I wasn't the only one. People began whispering and shifting their positions. The smell of smoke increased. I watched the musicians hastily pack up their instruments. I watched Leila try to keep pace with her rehearsed speech, readjust her glasses and begin again. Obviously the smoke smell had not penetrated through the crowd to where she stood.

Finally, a large man, his suit jacket removed to reveal suspenders over a white dress shirt and fat belly, came out of the foyer space shouting, "People! There's a fire!"

And then bedlam broke loose, people yelling, not knowing whether they should run toward the cloakroom to investigate or race toward the exit to escape. Most began rushing toward the front door. I stood still, fearful of a stampede. Somewhere along the line I'd lost Louise and Todd. And I still didn't see Evan. Or Mose.

"Everyone! Don't panic!" Leila screamed into the microphone. "Someone help me grab the pictures. Did someone call the police?"

"Someone call 911!"

"We have to get the artwork."

I flattened myself against the wall and waited for a chance to leave. Someone kept yelling, "The pictures! We need to get the pictures!"

Someone else said, "Don't worry about the pictures! Everyone get out."

"Try to be orderly."

"Watch it."

"Please, we all need to get out."

"Don't panic."

I heard the crashing of glass and realized someone must've tipped over the table of drinks, and this was proven to be true when I felt my feet wet in my thin-soled shoes. I heard cursing; someone yelled that 911 had been called. Seeing a gap, I made for the door.

And through all this, I saw neither Evan nor Mose. Once in the street in front of the gallery, no one seemed to be in any particular hurry to leave. It looked like a miniature of the inside of the gallery with people standing around, holding their wine, and inexplicably, a number milled around with heaped plates of food, remarking on the fire.

I was freezing in the thin black dress and hugged my arms. I didn't know what I was supposed to do. Grab a cab and head home? Wait for Evan? Fortunately, I still had my purse on my shoulder with my wallet and enough money to catch a cab home. I also had my cell phone. I checked to make sure it was turned on.

I went over and sat on the stoop of the building next door to the gallery, hugging my knees and watching. I heard sirens, and eventually a red fire truck and two police cars arrived and parked in front of the smoke-filled gallery.

By now a few of the revelers were leaving, grabbing cabs or making their ways to their parked cars. Some stayed, however, drinking wine and watching the fun. I sat and waited.

I was tired and felt smoky and dirty, and my dress was horribly wrinkled, but most of all I was cold. I was in this less-than-stellar condition when Louise and Todd approached.

"Marylee? We couldn't find you. We saw Evan."

"What happened?" I asked, rising and brushing off the back of my dress. I noticed a wide run in my black panty hose from sitting on the cement stoop.

"We don't know, I don't think anybody knows," Todd said. "Evan doesn't know. He apologizes."

Louise added, "We understand you were supposed to go for dinner with some of the gallery people? Well, Evan said that's not likely to happen now. We'd love for you to join us for dinner. Evan said he'd join us as soon as he can get away."

I was hugging my bare arms, teeth chattering. The street in front of the gallery had been blocked off by red fire trucks, and people still milled and talked.

"Evan recommended a good place that usually doesn't require reservations," she added.

Going out to dinner with Evan's parents was the last thing I felt like doing. That scented bubble bath and romance novel sounded much better. But I was so hungry that my stomach had been growling for at least the last half an hour. Wanting to fit into this slim black dress, all I'd had since breakfast was one cup of citrusy punch and two tiny baguette slices spread with Brie.

Maybe going out with Evan's parents would be in my best interest in my continuing quest to get answers. Maybe Louise and

Todd knew of Adam and Sonya Samuels. Or maybe I could find out if they were Evan's real parents. And what had happened to his sister.

"I would love to," I said, rubbing my arms. "But I'm really freezing. And I'm a mess."

"I think all of us are," Louise said. "None of us were able to get our coats. But, Todd, isn't Evan's coat in our backseat? He left it there a few days ago. Let's make a rush to the car and we'll all be warmer. I think there's even a blanket or two back there. We'll get that heater going."

I ran as best as I could in my pointy heels. We reached their car, a white four-door late-model sedan parked two blocks away.

Several people walked past us; a woman held an empty glass of wine. I had a vague idea she planned to keep it.

I got in the backseat and put Evan's jacket around my shoulders. It instantly made me warmer. It still held a faint trace of his aftershave. I felt so sad sitting there. I wanted, needed so much for Evan to be who he said he was. I needed for him to be a good Christian, a trustworthy man, not a monster, not a maniac, not a fire starter. But my mind spilled over with questions. And now tonight's fire was just a bit too coincidental. I leaned forward and spoke to Todd and

Louise in the front. "How did the fire start? Does anyone know?"

"Here's what I'm thinking," Todd said. "It was old wiring. Some of these buildings are so old they're just asking for trouble."

I thought about my own building, about the loose latch, about the bits of falling ceiling I'd found on the floor in my hallway. I'd swept them up, but was my place falling apart, too?

"Where was Evan when it started? I didn't see him," I said.

Louise turned around and faced me. "He's okay, thank God. I actually don't think anybody was hurt, which is a mercy. So, don't you worry, Evan's just fine."

But I wasn't finished. "Why was he back there when it started?"

"I'm not sure," Todd said. "Getting something last minute from his coat? I'm sure we'll find out. Wherever he was, Mose was there, too. Mose was the one who noticed the smoke."

Mose, the smoking man, I thought. And Evan, the arsonist's apprentice. I shook those thoughts out of my head. I was coming up with characters for a horror movie again.

I leaned back in the seat, put my hands in the pockets of the coat and fingered a roll of film in one and a folded piece of paper in the other.

The three of us talked a bit more about the fire, about old buildings and how it was a good thing no one was hurt and how we hoped the fire hadn't done too much damage. Louise worried about the artwork, and especially Evan's photographs, and I found myself thinking about the borrowed coat and the cashmere scarf and gloves. I'd somehow have to come up with the money to replace them. There goes my hardwood floors, I thought.

About twenty minutes later we began driving slowly past a restaurant. Todd said, "Is this the place Evan told us to go?"

Louise opened her purse and pulled out a piece of paper. "This looks like the place, dear."

Todd pulled the car into the parking lot of a brick-fronted Italian restaurant with stained-glass patterns in some of the windows.

I felt entirely less than glamorous as I trudged in with Evan's jacket, the run in my black nylons, my hair askew and feet still sticky from the wash of punch and wine all over the gallery floor.

I excused myself almost immediately and went to the ladies' room. The first thing I did was go into a stall and open up the paper from Evan's pocket. On it I read: *Danny M. Smythe* followed by a telephone number. I folded it up and put it back in the pocket.

Next, pulled off my black panty hose and shoved them in a garbage can. Aunt Rose had been full of practical advice and platitudes, and aside from the standard "Wear good underwear in case you're in a bus accident," she'd said that a woman attending a formal function should always carry an extra pair of panty hose in her purse. Before I put them on, however, I hobbled to a sink and wiped off my sticky feet with a wet paper towel. Then I pulled up the clean panty hose, put my shoes on, smoothed my dress. Near the hemline there were a few spots of dirt, which I got rid of with another damp paper towel.

My face was next. My mascara had wended its way in rivulets down my cheeks, making me look like a refugee from an eighties rock band. I wiped my face with another damp cloth, and applied fresh makeup. Finally, I decided to contend with my hair. Johanna's silver barrette had slid down my hair to cheekbone level. I took it out, combed my hair and attempted to fluff it up a bit, but the damp night air had hopelessly flattened it. So much for hot rollers. While I was refastening the barrette, my cell phone rang. I unzipped my little sparkly purse and scrounged for it.

"Marylee? It's Evan."

"Evan! What happened? Are you okay?" I leaned against the paper-towel dispenser.

"Nobody was hurt, and it doesn't even look like any of the artwork was damaged. Are you with my parents or did you go home?"

"I stayed with your parents."

"Oh." He seemed surprised at that. "I suggested they invite you out. I wasn't sure you'd do that."

"Well, I did. Is that okay?"

"Of course! I'm going to try to get away, but at this point I can't guarantee anything. Leila's having a fit."

"I bet."

"The bad news is that most of the coats are smoke damaged and some have been burned. It's just one of those things. It's nobody's fault."

"Oh." I thought again of my expensive borrowed outerwear. "But how did it start?"

"I don't know that yet."

We said goodbye after I promised to tell his parents that he would call them later. He wanted to make this up to me, and I said that was okay. These things happen. It's nobody's fault. But I wondered about that last statement even as I said it. *It's nobody's fault?*

I combed my hair and refastened the barrette.

I realized just how overdressed I was in this restaurant when a woman came into the ladies' room in jeans and a baggy Catamounts hockey hoodie. Plus, I felt a little odd having dinner with a date's parents. This wasn't something you did on a first date. But this wasn't a date, I had to keep reminding myself.

There was a basket of bread on the table when I returned, and places set for four. I hung Evan's jacket on the chair behind me and sat down across from Louise.

"Evan called while I was in the ladies' room. He's not sure he'll be able to get here. He'll try, though. That's what he said."

Louise leaned forward. "Oh, we should phone him, Todd. Did you bring the cell?"

"I think I left it in the car."

I rummaged in my purse. "You can borrow mine."

Todd said, "I don't think we should disturb him, Louise, if he's busy with the police. We'll talk to him later."

Louise asked, "Do they know what started

the fire? Did he say?"

"He didn't know. It sounds like they got everything out in time."

Todd took a roll from the basket and buttered it. Louise unfolded her napkin and placed it on her lap. "I hope he's able to join us."

I took a piece of the bread, which was fresh and warm, buttered it and ate it. During the time I'd been nibbling on nibblies at the reception, I'd been exceedingly hungry. Now everything tasted like cardboard, because what was Evan doing with Danny M. Smythe's phone number in his pocket?

The waitress came and took our orders. I'd had little time to look at the menu, so I quickly ordered chicken marinara, the first thing I saw.

We talked a bit about the fire until our salads arrived. Todd reiterated his position that it was faulty wiring. I wanted this to be true, but I wasn't sure. One thing my aunt had been fond of saying was that there was no such thing as coincidence.

When our salads came, Louise peppered me with questions about myself, which I answered with as much candidness as I could. I grew up in Portland, I told them, but when the aunt who raised me died, I decided to move here.

"Why?" she asked. Obviously Evan hadn't shared my history with his parents, and that was a good thing.

"Oh." I stopped. "I don't know. Always wanted to come out east, I guess."

"And you left family back in Portland to come out here all by yourself?"

I nodded. Part of that story was true. I didn't leave family back there, but I did come out here all by myself. But I was getting tired of talking about me. It was a topic that required too much explanation.

"Tell me about when Evan was a boy," I said. "I never got to hear the end of Leila's introduction." *Tell me,* I wanted to ask, *if you're his real parents or his foster parents. Tell me about his fire-starting sister who's in jail.*

Louise brightened. "He was quite the boy. What an imagination he had. I always knew he'd be some sort of artist. He just had that in him."

"He was always coming up with stories," Todd said.

Louise agreed.

"Got that boy in trouble a time or two," Todd said. "His stories did."

"How so?" I asked as nonchalantly as I could.

"Oh, you know, little boy stuff. Always so

curious about how the world worked. That's the sort of stuff that got him in trouble."

"Taking things apart," Louise answered. "Not realizing that when you take apart a watch, for example, you can't always get it back together again."

"What about fires?" I asked, balancing a tiny round tomato on my fork. "He has that one really stunning picture of a fire."

"Fires are his specialty," Louise said.

The little tomato fell off my fork. His specialty was fires? How could she say that with a straight face, a smile even?

"What do you mean fire is his specialty?" I kept my voice level.

"His photography. Fire has always been one of his favorite subjects."

"What about when he was younger?" I asked. "Were fires his specialty when he was younger?"

Louise frowned, seemed flustered. "Evan didn't get his first camera until he was in high school. I'm not sure when he took his first picture of a fire. Is that what you're asking?"

The waitress brought our main courses. This was going to be a long meal, and I wasn't hungry. I cut a piece of chicken and the sauce sputtered all over the table. Luckily none landed on my clothes. "Right.

That's what I'm asking."

"Not that we know of." Todd winked at me. Like father like son, I thought.

We managed to get through the main course, but all of us declined dessert, which made me happy. I just needed to get home. Evan never did show up for dinner and while that didn't entirely surprise me, it felt awkward, somewhat, being with his parents.

FIFTEEN

The first thing I did when Louise and Todd dropped me off at my apartment, even before I checked my phone messages, was to run a hot bath with plenty of fragrant bubbles. My entire self needed nothing more than to soak away all the niggling questions. So much for my fact-finding mission. I'd ended up with more questions than answers.

I shrugged out of my black dress. It needed triage more than dry cleaning. And then there was the little matter of the jacket. Evan had said some of them had been burned, and those that weren't were smoke damaged. Great. Just what I needed, to spend all this month's profits on wrecked borrowed designer clothes.

Todd and Louise had insisted that I wear Evan's jacket home, and I dug out the folded slip of paper. With the tub water running, I dialed the number for Danny M.

Smythe. While it was ringing, I realized I had no idea what I was going to say to this person. *Hello, Danny Smythe? Were you responsible for the fire that killed my parents? Were you working with Evan's sister? Who are you, anyway, and why does your name keep coming up?*

The phone rang twice, three times, and on the fourth ring it went to voice mail. I sat down on the end of my bed when I heard where it originated.

"You've reached the voice mail of Martin Smythe. Please leave your name and number after the beep."

Gently I hung up the phone without saying anything. So, what did this mean? That Marty was lying? That he *did* know who Danny Smythe was? That they were related? That he was protecting him, somehow? I put the phone back in its cradle and then saw that I had a message.

It was from Jared. I clicked on it.

"Marylee? I found out a few things you might want to know. I did a check of government records. Your name was legally changed in Portland, Oregon, from Marybelle Rose Samuels to Marylee Rose Simson. I was even able to get a copy of the document in case you want to see it."

I sat down at my kitchen table and put

my head in my hands. Why hadn't my aunt told me this? I got up, went into my bathroom and turned off the water. Obviously, my scented bubble bath and a romance novel would have to wait. I was restless to relax. I'd never be able to concentrate on a book. Also, I was angry. I paced my kitchen floor and felt like punching things. This was my life! How dare she do this to me! I put a hand to my forehead, pulled out a chair and, with a groan, sat down at my kitchen table. The mother of all headaches was threatening. I sat for a few moments until my anger subsided a bit. Then, mentally I checked off what I knew for sure:

1. My name is really Marybelle Samuels. (Great. What a name to be saddled with.)
2. Evan's parents are his real parents, at least his father is his father. Maybe. Or at least there is a strong family resemblance that no one can deny.
3. Evan's "specialty" is fires. And his sister is currently in prison for arson.
4. It was Mose who watched me from the bus shelter.
5. Both Evan and Mose were conve-

niently nowhere to be found when the fire started in the gallery tonight.

6. Evan had a picture of my parents all along and didn't tell me.
7. Danny M. Smythe stole (maybe) from my parents' store and is related to Marty Smythe. (Or at least that's what the phone seems to indicate. But then, how can I really trust Evan?)
8. I have at least one relative here according to the obituary I'd seen in the library. Gabby Samuels is my father's sister-in-law. (Maybe I should call her? Go see her?)
9. Someone is trying to kill me. (Maybe. But why?)

Instead of a long fragrant bubble bath, I quickly showered away the smoke smell and climbed into some warm flannel pajamas. Clean, I felt better. I'd figure all of this out. I grabbed one of my aunt Rose's quilts, wrapped myself up in it and sat on my couch. Then, filled with a kind of strange uneasiness that I couldn't define, I wandered around my small apartment, touching things. I guess I was feeling rather disjointed. Who was I? It was as if by touching my things I could assure myself that I was real and belonged here.

"How come I know so little about you?" I picked up the picture of my parents and looked down at them. "And here's something else — don't you think it's a bit of a coincidence that Evan, the guy I just happen to meet in a coffee shop, has something to do with me and *you?* Isn't that a bit of a stretch?" I shook my head, puzzling over that and put the photo back down. None of this made sense.

And then I blinked. My brand-new deadbolted door to my balcony was unlocked! On legs that felt as heavy as cement, I walked over to it. Yes, the door was unlocked.

I opened the door to the balcony and felt a rush of cold. I stepped out in bare feet. My wicker rocking chair was gone. I stood there in my pajamas, the cold wind biting at my eyes and I said something over and over that sounded like, "Oh no, oh no, oh no."

It was truly gone. I looked over the railing to my car below, but the chair had not magically flown over the railing and landed in the alley down below. Somehow I got myself back into my kitchen, relocked the door and picked up the phone. It was time for 911. "Someone is trying to kill me! Someone is trying to torment me and I don't know why!" I wanted to shriek. Instead, I said very calmly, "I wish to report a burglary."

Before the police came, I had the foresight to change out of my flannel pajamas and into sweatpants and a hoodie. I knew they would ask if anything else had been taken, so I did a quick check of my jewelry box, which contained some fine pieces that had belonged to my aunt in addition to the costume stuff. But everything was there, including a couple of twenties that I'd left on my kitchen counter. Ten minutes later, my back door buzzer sounded and I opened it up to Jared and a woman officer in a uniform.

"Jared!" I said.

"What is it, Marylee? What happened? Are you okay?" he asked. "Did you get my message?"

I nodded. "Yeah, that's the least of my problems now. My chair's gone. From my balcony." I tried to keep that shrieky tone out of my voice. I tried to keep my hands still at my sides.

I showed them my porch, the new lock, and I explained that up until a few days ago there had just been a slide bolt on this door, but when I kept coming home and the door was unlocked or open, I replaced it with a true dead bolt.

"Who installed this?" Jared asked.

"I did."

He raised his eyebrows. "You did?"

"I'm pretty handy with a hammer and chisel."

"I remember," he said.

He was examining it carefully, while I jabbered on about the fire in the gallery and me not being who I am and someone trying to keep me a long time ago. I was spilling it all out fast.

The female officer, who introduced herself as Nell, suggested that we sit down so I could go over everything, from the moment I came home to when I discovered the burglary.

Jared's eyes screwed together and I could tell he was trying to make sense of my late-night ramblings. I felt like crying. Nell took notes while I talked. I tried to get things in order this time. I told them everything, including all about the Samuelses and my parents and Danny Smythe being related somehow to Marty, who was in one of my classes, and when I mentioned the fire that had killed my parents nearly thirty years ago, Nell's eyebrows shot up.

"Did you know about that?" I asked.

She shook her head. "Before my time. But

I heard the rumors. My dad was a police officer, too. There are a lot of us who'd like to put that whole thing to bed."

After I'd gone over my story a bunch more times, Jared got up and examined the French door and the porch. They shone their flashlights against the railings, looking, he said, for any indication that a ladder had recently been propped alongside it. They found nothing.

A few moments later we were downstairs and looking around the alleyway. Jared checked the Dumpster, but the chair wasn't there. They looked at my car. If my chair had been thrown over the railing, it would quite possibly have hit my car. But my little Saturn was in perfect condition. It wasn't even honking by itself.

Then we were back inside and standing in my hallway. They were especially interested in my security system.

Nell asked, "Have you given these numbers out to anyone? Does anyone else know your security code?"

I said no, not even my best friend Johanna knew my security code.

Jared bent down and ran his hands gently on the floor where I'd found the bits of dust the previous week.

"This old house," I said fisting and unfisting my hands. "I think it shakes every time a truck goes by. Maybe I never should have bought this old place, what a white elephant . . ."

"No," Jared said, straightening and looking at the ceiling above where we stood. "I think this might be something else. Do you have a step stool handy?"

I went and fetched the one I keep in the kitchen. He stood on the top step and with a small pocketknife, he picked away at the ceiling.

"Here," Jared said, stepping down. "Here's the culprit." He showed me a small round disk and then plopped it into a baggie. I couldn't think what it was and asked.

"Digital camera," he said. "Someone installed this. It would give a clear view to you when you punch in or change your security code. Mystery solved."

"What!" I hugged my arms around me. I had begun to shiver. "Why would someone do this, just so they could come in and steal lawn furniture? It doesn't make sense." My teeth chattered.

"Let's go sit down again," he said. "Let's talk this through." He led me into my kitchen and the three of us sat down. While it lay on the table between us in the plastic bag, Jared explained how this little camera might work. It looked like an eye, and I felt exposed. Someone had been watching me with this eye. But why? Who was I and what did people want with me?

Jared explained that somewhere, in another building perhaps, was a small recorder where the camera could be accessed remotely.

I said, "I don't get it. I don't get it."

"You ever heard of WI-FI?" Nell said. "Same idea. The pictures themselves would be at another remote location, an apartment or across the back alley perhaps. Or even through the walls. How well do you know your neighbors?" she asked.

"Pretty well," I answered. "Most of them are old. I can't imagine them doing this or why they even would." I thought of the elderly couple that lived beside me in the apartment above the ski shop. They were nice, stuck to themselves and I couldn't imagine them doing anything like this. On the other side in the apartment over the coffee shop was a young married couple.

I thought about something and then said, "What about down below the front of my building?" And then I told them about the man I'd seen smoking in front of my apartment. They followed me to the front window and when I pulled the blinds back, we got a clear view of the bus shelter.

"I was up here and saw someone smoking. And I have an idea of who it was, but I don't know why he would want to spy on me, or steal my chair. Why would someone want to steal my chair?"

I told them that I thought I had seen Mose down there, leaning against the shelter and smoking. Nell wrote down his name, and then a few minutes later I found myself down below in the dark looking at them shine their flashlights all around the bus shelter.

Jared asked me how I knew Mose and I said he and Evan were doing some work for me. "Could he be behind this?"

They found a few cigarette butts, which they put in plastic baggies.

"But it makes perfect sense," I said. "Who better to know about remote cameras but a photographer?" But, now that I thought about it, was I sure? I shook my head. "But I'm not totally sure it's him. It could be." It was late and I was dead tired, my head hurt and I was talking too much and too long. Tears began escaping from the corners of my eyes. I didn't want to be this way, sniveling female, but there you have it.

"We'll check it all out," Jared said. "I know how unnerving this whole thing must be, but there's another possibility that we need to consider, too, and that's that the camera lens has been here for a while and is inoperative."

"But that doesn't explain my door being opened and my chair gone. Why would someone do that? Steal from me?"

"Maybe to frighten you," Nell suggested.

"Well, it's working big-time."

Nell touched my hand and Jared asked if there was anyone who could come and stay with me.

I said no. I thought of Johanna, but I didn't feel like driving all the way out there in the middle of the night. I shook my head and said I would be fine. I'd make sure everything was locked up tight.

Just before they left, Jared handed me his business card and told me to call him anytime, day or night.

Numbly, I nodded.

My name is Marybelle Samuels. I was named for my maternal grandmother, Marybelle West. My mother didn't want to name me Marybelle. Interestingly enough, she wanted me called Marylee. She'd come across the name in a novel once, and liked it. So, in a way, she got her wish. Along with changing my name, Aunt Rose legally changed her own name from Rose West to Rose Carlson. She did all this to keep me safe from the person who killed my parents. And she was convinced that it was not just a random arson, but premeditated murder. She had the proof, the ledger book she'd kept with her lawyer. The day after the fire in the gallery — a fire I was now convinced had been started by Mose — I learned all this from Gabby Samuels, my father's sister.

And yet, here I was, three days after the fire in the gallery sitting in the passenger seat of Evan's silver SUV in my navy cords and a leather jacket belonging to Johanna's sister. Johanna had helped me dress again. How I ended up here was quite simple. The morning after the fire in the gallery, Evan had called me at the store and invited me to go with him for a drive up the lake to watch him take pictures. Well, I had to return his jacket, plus I still had questions. That's what I told myself.

Evan was sorry about the previous evening and wanted to make it up to me. He knew of this wonderful out-of-the-way restaurant and would love to take me there. Was there any way I could get the time off from the store? He knew I closed at five on Wednesdays. But was there any way we could leave a little earlier that day? Say three? He really wanted to see me, needed to see me, was how he put it.

Needed to see me. "Yes," I said, my hand gripping the receiver. "I'd love to." How was it that I couldn't say no to him? I couldn't quite trust him — not really — yet I couldn't say no.

I called Barbara at home and she said she could come in, no problem, and then she asked me how I'd enjoyed my date with Jared.

"My *what?*"

"Oh, hmm, he told me that you and he were going out for coffee. Maybe that, uh, um hasn't happened yet. Or maybe he hasn't asked you?"

"No."

"He talks about you all the time."

"Oh." How did I feel about that? Jared was a nice guy. Lots of girls would be crazy about Jared. Maybe he could even grow on me if I gave him half a chance. It would be good to go out with a guy I could totally trust, wouldn't it? A guy with an ordinary past.

"You want to get a coffee to go?" Evan's questions brought me abruptly back to the present. "I was thinking we could get a couple of coffees at the drive-through, on the corner," he said. "I really need one."

"Sure, sounds great," I said. He was wearing the jacket with the pockets, the one I'd had for two days. I looked over at him, at the strong jawline, the way he crinkled his eyebrows together when he talked, the way the right side of his mouth rose in a half smile when he said certain words. Today he wore jeans and tan boots. Underneath his jacket he had on a plaid flannel shirt. Only Evan could pull off a plaid flannel shirt without looking like someone on the lam from the fashion police. The fact that I noticed what he was wearing down to the minutest detail gave me pause. I could barely remember what Jared even looked like.

We lined up at the drive-through and Evan turned to me, concern in his face. "I'm glad we have this time together. I'm really sorry the gallery opening turned out the way it did. I was so hoping it would be a good time."

"That's okay, really. It's not your fault." But even as I said it, I wondered if it somehow was his fault, even indirectly. Mose was certainly involved, Mose who stood down below my apartment and looked up at me.

"Is your jacket okay?"

"It's fine. I picked it up yesterday. It

hardly even smells like smoke."

"That's good then." We were at the drive-through window and he handed me my coffee.

As we pulled away, I took a breath, decided to tell him. "Something bad happened to me. I didn't tell you. On the night of the fire in the gallery someone broke into my apartment."

He turned to me, wide-eyed. "Marylee! Are you okay? Was anything taken? Any of your stock? You should have called me."

"No, I'm fine, really I am, and whoever it was only took a chair from my balcony. That's all." Evan slowed to a stop. In front of us on the sidewalk a woman was running with one of those jogging baby strollers.

"They only took a chair? What did the police say?" He took a sip of his coffee, and placed his paper cup into the holder between the seats.

"They're looking into it. They, um, they found something else." I hesitated. "They think someone might be spying on me."

He took the ramp to I-98 North. "What do you mean someone is spying on you? You mean like looking in your windows?"

I shook my head. "The police found a hidden camera in my hallway."

He turned to me. "Marylee! Are you serious? What do you mean they found a camera? What kind of camera? Where?"

I described the camera Jared had found with as much detail as I could remember. I told him that Jared had suggested that it was remotely operated.

"The police could come to me," Evan said, maneuvering around a transport truck. "I probably could source it. Do they have any idea why? That would also be right up my alley."

I looked at him. "I bet. Yours and Mose's both."

"Did the police give you any indication what they may have been looking for? Or why someone was doing this?"

"None." Outside, the road sped past in a haze of brown trees and gray sky. "They did suggest that it may have been there a long time. Maybe it had nothing to do with me." Yeah, right. And if you believe that, I've got a bridge for sale. . . . "They're also looking at previous tenants." I took a sip of my coffee and shivered slightly.

Evan picked up his coffee, seemed to consider it before putting it back again without taking a sip. "I worry about you. There are just too many crazy people out there."

I looked down at my hands, then over at

Evan, then out the passenger window. I didn't know what to think. I didn't know what to think about anything.

We were quiet for a while, but I could see that Evan was mulling something over in his mind. After we had gone another mile, he said, "There's another reason I invited you out today."

I looked at him sharply.

"I wanted to tell you I've done a bit more sleuthing in that book you left with me. I've gone over it page by page. I don't know for sure who it was, but someone was systematically helping himself from the cash register at Samuels Hardware. I've crunched the numbers, all the numbers. I have the proof now."

"Could that be the person named Danny Smythe?"

"Maybe. I wish we had more to go on. A picture would help. I found Danny Smythe through an online directory that I had access to from my police work. I'm not sure they know I still have access, but it comes in handy sometimes. I found out that Danny Smythe is listed at the same address as Martin Smythe."

I nodded. I already knew this. I'd seen the note in Evan's pocket. I'd gotten the answering-machine message.

Evan drummed his finger on the steering wheel. "It's my opinion that this Marty character that you know may know Danny's whereabouts. It could be a nephew or something."

I picked up my still-too-hot coffee and took a sip. "He worked for my parents," I said.

When he looked over at me with eyebrows raised, I said, "You're not the only hotshot detective in all of this." I tried a bit of a grin, but worried that it came across more as a smirk.

I told him that two days ago I'd met my father's sister, Gabby. "She told me all this."

"You met her?"

I nodded. But that was all. I didn't tell him how that meeting had progressed. I didn't tell him the whole story. I didn't tell him everything. I didn't tell him how I'd driven over to visit G. Samuels after work.

The address I'd found in the phone book was for a three-story town house in the center of a block of three-story town houses. I parked in front, and it wasn't until I was ringing the doorbell that I realized what I was doing, and thought maybe I should have come here with some sort of a plan. Or at least have figured out the first sentence that would come out of my mouth.

And so when I found myself standing in front of a tall, elegant woman in her mid-sixties, I was tongue-tied.

"Yes?" she said. "Can I help you?"

"I'm here to ask about Adam and Sonya Samuels."

She stopped, looked at me for a long time before she said, "You're the child."

I think I was prepared for anything but that.

She said again, "You're the child who went away with Rose." Her voice had a silky quality to it. It was the kind of voice you could listen to all day long. I absolutely could not think of what to say.

She spoke. "I would recognize you anywhere. You have the classic West face."

"The what face?" I managed to ask.

"The West face, high cheekbones. Your mother's face. If . . ." She stopped. "You are the child. Come in," Gabby said. "We have a lot to talk about."

At her bidding, I followed her inside into a nicely laid out albeit modest town house. The walls, carpets and lush furniture were in various shades of beige and white. It struck me as regal. There was a softness about the place, which seemed to match the persona of Gabby Samuels. We sat on couches in the living room and faced each other.

She said, "I wondered when you would come back."

"You did?" I felt drawn to her gentle spirit like a dog in summer to a bowl of cool water.

She nodded. "Let me just look at you."

I was still too shocked to find many words. My mouth was dry. I coughed. She went and got me a glass of water and placed it on the glass coffee table between us.

Then she leaned forward and touched my face. "I should explain," she said. "Your father and my husband were brothers. Sonya and I were close. The four of us were. When they died, it was like my whole world collapsed. Nothing was the same after that." She paused, drew in a breath. "Your name is Marybelle. Your name has a story," she said and then she told me the story of my name, how I was named for my grandmother and how my mother wanted me to be called Marylee. I sat back and listened to the story. I had so many questions.

"Your husband . . ." I didn't finish my sentence.

"Killed himself? That's the story, but it's not what happened. I will go to my grave knowing that's not what happened." She shook her head. "He was murdered. He was convinced that the deaths of Adam and Sonya weren't a case of a bunch of boys setting the place on fire by mistake. It was a purposeful murder, and they were the targets. If it *was* kids, then there was a mastermind behind them."

This statement made me choke. I thought of Evan and his sister, the one in jail for arson. I had to ask. "Do you know the name Evan Baxter?"

It took her a while, but she shook her head. "That name's not familiar to me. I'm sorry."

"What about Danny Smythe?"

She cocked her head, looked thoughtful. "I remember him. He worked for Adam and Sonya. As I remember, he was good to the family after the fire."

"How was he good to the family?"

"Helpful. Especially at the store. The store was burned down, but for days afterward he helped to organize the papers and books and what stock remained. I think he did all of this as a favor to the family, because Rose, who, along with my husband, Warren, were the beneficiaries of the company, told him that it might be a while before they could sort things out and pay him for this work. He said he wouldn't accept any payment. So, it was Rose and Danny who worked long hours sorting things through. Poor Danny had been through some personal tragedy in his own life, yet he was willing to do this."

"What kind of personal tragedy?"

"His wife left him, I believe. I don't know all the details. I think Rose did. I had this feeling at the time that Rose was falling for him. I worried for Rose, because, of course, Danny was married at the time, even though there were problems there. It wasn't too long after his wife left that the store burned down. I didn't want Rose getting hurt. I have a feeling she may have been. Though we never talked about it."

I opened my mouth to say something, and didn't. In all our years in Portland, Rose had never spoken about a love interest. And despite being attractive and smart, she rarely dated. Had she been hurt by Danny Smythe?

"And then she left with you. At first we were frantic. We had no idea why, of course." Gabby leaned back in her chair and put a hand to her chest. "Oh, my, this happened so long ago. These are things I haven't spoken about in a long time." Gabby paused and her voice broke. "A week later Rose contacted us. You and she were safe. That's all she told us. We never knew why. All she said was that you'd be safe now. And that she'd taken some sort of evidence with her."

I thought about the ledger. "She never told you what it was?"

Gabby shook her head. "No. It was all so secretive. Maybe once every couple of years she would send a picture. That's about it. I've saved them all."

Gabby went and got a box, and I looked at pictures of Rose and me from various years in Portland. She turned to me and said, "Do you have any idea what this evidence was?"

"I might." I told her about the book I'd found. "It sort of proves that someone was systematically stealing from the store."

Gabby looked surprised. "I didn't know this."

"I don't think anyone knew. But I think it may have been Danny Smythe."

And then I'd told her the theory that I'd been working on during the past little while, that someone had been stealing from the business and it might have been Danny Smythe. I'd also suggested that he'd been confronted by my parents to give it back, but instead had coerced a bunch of neighbor kids to burn the store down.

Evan held his coffee in his left hand now

and the steering wheel with the other, and I continued with my story. ". . . So my new aunt Gabby told me that Danny Smythe worked for my parents and that he was a model employee."

He frowned. "Sometimes things are not what they seem."

"Tell me about it." I looked away from him. I watched the trees, the water. I'd spent a lifetime where nothing was as it seemed. We went over a bump and coffee sloshed onto Evan's hand.

"Drat," he said. "Whew. That's hot."

I grabbed a Kleenex from my purse and gave it to him. He tried mopping up with one hand, but clearly was unable to do that and steer at the same time, so I wiped his hand and the steering wheel. Our hands touched, and he held mine for an instant and looked at me before he let go.

A little while later he said to me, "You're quiet. You're thinking about the fire. I can tell."

His question startled me until I realized he was talking about the fire in the gallery. "Maybe. It is upsetting."

"I didn't want to tell you this, because I didn't want you to worry, but I guess I should. The police are pretty convinced it was arson. I talked with a cop just this morning."

I nearly spilled my coffee. "They think it was *arson?*" I thought about the police at my house the other night. Were the two connected? How could they be?

He nodded. "They found a rag soaked with gasoline. But fortunately, and I'm sure God may have had something to do with this, the rag was damp and didn't ignite. Only smoked. We can be thankful for that."

"So, it was arson?" I still couldn't get my mind to bend itself around that fact.

"That's what they're saying."

"Well," I said. "Good thing you and Mose were back there then."

He must've heard something in my tone because he turned to me suddenly. Then he looked back at the road. But I wasn't ready to let it go. "You were back there when the fire started, right?"

"I was. But I didn't see anyone come in with a jerrican. I wish I could have been more helpful to the police."

"But what were you doing back there in the first place?" I really wanted to know. It made no sense that he and Mose just happened to be back there at the same time — especially Mose.

"Okay," he said, grinning. "Here's why I was back there. I knew I would be speaking soon, so I thought I'd hit the restroom before zero hour."

"Oh."

"When I came out I smelled smoke. Mose was disappointed he didn't get a better look at the man he saw running from the gallery."

"Really? He saw someone running?" How convenient, I thought.

"With a red jerrican. But he didn't get a good look. He's working with the police now."

"And the police don't have any idea who it was?"

He shook his head. "Right now the rumors are flying. There's even one that Leila set it herself because she wants the insurance money."

"Could that be true?"

"Not at all. Man," he said, looking ahead of him. "The light's no good. I've got this special place I want to show you, some trees, and I thought today would be the perfect day to capture the firelight in the branches, but we're getting clouds. Do you see them?"

I did. "Do you want to go back, then?"

His eyes went wide. "No, not at all. No, that's not the purpose of this trip. The purpose of this trip is to make up for that lost dinner of the other night."

He grinned and I looked at the way that little bit of his hair curled over his collar. And yet . . . I looked away from him and said, "That picture of my parents. You said you wanted to continue to work on it?"

"Yes, I have some ideas on more places to look."

"And you can't do any more work on it without my original, the only copy, the one I have. I have the one and only copy, right?"

"Right. But, only if you want to trust me with it."

I looked away. I wanted to cry. I was so tired of being lied to. He had another copy. I'd seen it on his desk.

"How long has Mose been with you?" I asked at one point.

"Around six years."

I looked toward him. "Do you know him really well?"

"He's quiet and is really talented. He helps me with the work we do for the police. He's an excellent forensic investigator. Got a good eye for some things. Knows his stuff. Knows his cameras."

"Knows his cameras." I said it so quietly that I didn't think Evan heard me. Knows his cameras, knows all about his cameras, especially little remote ones you operate from bus shelters across from where you've planted the original. A few minutes later I asked Evan to tell me about his childhood. "Leila started to talk about you the other night, but never got to finish the introduction. Your story seems interesting."

And so, for the rest of the trip to the trees, he told me about a very ordinary childhood growing up on the outskirts of Burlington, just his sister and him. It was a childhood filled with Sunday school and church camp and youth group and mission trips. But, was this rendition a bit too sanitized? No teenage rebellion, as I'd had? No struggles with church and God, as I'd had? He also conveniently never mentioned that his sister was in prison. At one point I asked, "Did you ever set fires when you were a kid?"

He looked over at me and pushed his glasses back on his nose. "What do you mean, like campfires? At camp?"

"Never mind." I looked away. "I don't know what I mean."

"Marylee, you're acting strange. Are you sure you're all right?"

"I'm fine."

When we finally got to the trees, I could see why he'd wanted to photograph this particular landscape. Three lone, branchless trees stuck out like skeleton hands under the cloudy sky. It would make a good cover of a book: *The Arsonist's Apprentice.* I shook those thoughts from my brain as he helped me out of his SUV. And once out, he did not let go. We walked toward the trees hand in hand. Despite all my misgivings, I was happy to be with him. I marveled at that. That I could doubt someone so intensely, yet trust him. It didn't make sense.

As I stood there I was taken back to that time along the lake where he'd excitedly photographed the sun on the boathouse roof. I watched again as he set up shot after shot. He was watching the trees, the clouds, the scrub brush, the wind in the trees. I watched him. I couldn't stop watching him. Every so often he'd turn and wink at me.

Later, in the restaurant, he told me that even though he hadn't had the firelight the way he'd wanted, he thought the pictures would be pretty good. The restaurant was everything he'd said it would be. It was out of the way, delicious food, rustic and romantic. Against the far wall was a huge stone fireplace, a real one, which burned actual logs. We talked across our candlelight dinner. Keep it on safe subjects, I told myself. I spent a lot of time telling him about the paper my aunt had made. He seemed quite fascinated with that. I promised to show him some samples sometime. He said he would like that. By the time we finished off with cheesecake and coffee, our meal ended up being three hours long. In the course of that three hours we'd talked about art, church, politics and music.

On the way out to his SUV he again took my hand. I wanted to trust him so much it made my stomach hurt.

"I enjoyed tonight," he said when we'd turned onto the highway to Burlington.

"So did I," I said.

"A lot," he said.

"A lot," I said.

"There's just one thing."

"Yes?"

"I wish you could trust me, Marylee," he said. "I know you've been hurt. I can see it in your eyes every time you look at me, how hurt you've been, but I want you to know that I'm someone you can trust."

I looked away from him out of the window at the dark woods that passed by my window.

Too soon we were at my back door. I quickly reached to open my own car door to let myself out. I needed to get up to my apartment and think about everything.

"Wait!" he called, grinning. "Don't open the door. Let me get it for you."

He jumped out of the car, came around, and very gallantly opened my door and took both my hands to help me up. And then I was standing in front of him, and suddenly his arms were around me and I found myself being very gently leaned against the car door frame. With the door still open and beeping behind us, he touched my face with his hand, and for a moment looked at me. Sounds seemed to intensify; the lights seemed to get softer. And then he kissed me.

And if I had forgotten to ask all my important questions before, they were now completely gone from my mind.

Sixteen

All the rest of the evening, through the night and into the next morning, I thought about Evan. I remembered our kiss. I replayed it a hundred times.

In the morning, I dressed carefully for work, knowing we might see each other in the coffee shop. I gave my hair a few more minutes under the blow dryer, frowning a few times at it. I really should get highlights. First chance I get, I'll do just that.

Evan and I ended up standing next to each other while we waited for our coffees. Well, maybe we planned it that way, or maybe he planned it that way. Or maybe I did, I don't know. But while we stood there, he excitedly told me about an e-mail he'd gotten last night. One of his stock photos was going to be used on the cover of a book. He told me all this while I just stood looking up into his eyes.

"I'll call you," he promised when we both

realized it was time to get to our respective stores.

"I look forward to it," I said.

He winked. And I wondered once again if I was falling for the wrong man, a man who would ultimately hurt me. I had to remind myself of that as I looked at the crinkly places beside his eyes.

At lunchtime there was an e-mail from him. One of his customers was an actor in the community theater, and had given him two tickets for a play on Friday. Would I be interested in going?

Sure, I typed back. *Sounds like fun.*

After work that day, as I made my way upstairs to my apartment, I could hear the phone in the kitchen ringing. Evan? I raced to unlock my door and press the new four-digit security code. I was able to grab the phone just before it went to voice mail.

"Marylee?"

"Yes," I said, breathless.

"This is Jared."

Jared. "Oh, hi, Jared."

"I wanted to phone about your chair."

"Did you find it? Did you find out what happened to it?"

"No. That's just it. I checked a lot of pawn shops, places like that, and we can't find it. We've questioned neighbors and no one saw a thing."

"Oh."

"I'm not sure what to say about it other than we're still working on it. Well, I'm still working on it. Also, I don't think that it was Mose down there on the nights in question."

"Oh?"

"He has a solid alibi."

"Oh."

"Uh, there's something else, another reason I called. I know this is last moment, but I was wondering if tonight would be a good time to, um, have that coffee we promised each other."

We promised each other coffee? "Jared, I just don't think I can make it tonight."

"Some other time, then."

"Yeah."

I opened up a can of soup and set it on the stove. Something in the picture of my parents caught my eye. I ran my fingers along the side where that elusive shaded something was, that thing I'd never been able to figure out. Was it the side of a building? Trees? And why did looking at this suddenly make me think of Evan?

But then I wondered if maybe I was thinking about Evan because for the past two days everything had made me think of Evan.

I picked up the picture from the kitchen table and looked at it. As I ran my finger along the side, I remembered again the afternoon when Evan had captured the firelight off the metal roof of the boat shed. I poured chicken-noodle soup into a bowl. Could this bit of shading be the shed that Evan had photographed when I was with him?

I would go there right now, I decided. It wasn't too late and I could use a walk. I would walk the mile or so down the lakefront until I came to the boathouse again. Maybe this was important. I called Johanna and left a message on her machine.

"Hey, I'm off on an adventure. I'd love for you to come along. There's this old boathouse way up past North Beach, and I'm on my way there now. Anyway, if you get back, that's where I am. I've missed you. We need to talk. So much has happened that I haven't told you about."

It looked like rain, so I laced up my boots and put on a waterproof jacket.

Then I got in my car, headed up toward North Beach and parked in the same place I'd parked when I'd met up with Evan.

I hadn't gone half a mile when I also wished I'd remembered an umbrella. The sky was starting to spit a nasty rain. But I was on the beach now and more than halfway there already. To my left, the lake spread out like slow-moving black oil. The rocks were dark and slippery, the edges of them crusted with wet foam. At one point I nearly slipped as my feet came upon a bit of ice. But I kept going.

It was as cold and still as a graveyard and I could smell snow in the air. I could see my breath and hear my boots crunching on the rough beachfront. I was thankful for the lack of wind. Any breeze, no matter how slight, and I'd be freezing as opposed to just plain cold.

And then I stopped. Was that another set of boots crunching on the rocks behind me? I turned. No one was there. I went back to my trek. Through the trees, I could almost see the shed in the distance. I hadn't gone more than a few steps when I again heard the sound of someone walking behind me. But, as before, when I turned, no one was there. I kept walking and ignored the sound, figuring it to be some acoustic illusion, made by the still air, the water and sleet quietly hitting rocks. Maybe this had happened before.

But I couldn't ignore it for long. There was someone behind me, beside me now. To my right were thick trees and bushes. Was there someone keeping step with me off to my right? I stopped very suddenly, and in a split second the sound of walking in the trees stopped as well.

I had two options. I could turn around and go back the way I'd come or I could keep on going and find refuge in the shed. But if I turned around whoever was following me could turn around, too. And if I found refuge in the shed, would I just be a sitting duck?

I felt trapped between the trees and the lake. I decided to press on toward the shed. When I got there, I'd see if I could get inside, dig to the bottom of my backpack for my cell phone and call someone. But who? Evan? I couldn't trust him. Johanna? But she wasn't answering her phone. Gabby? I'd call Gabby. I'd get inside, out of this wet miserableness, and call Gabby. Provided I could get inside. Maybe I should stop right now in the rain and dig out my cell from the bottom of my backpack. Oh, why didn't I keep my cell phone in my pocket like normal people?

It was raining harder now; thick, dense drops splatted against the beach stones. I was cold, I was wet and someone was following me, quite possibly the person who had wanted to kill me all along. I was running now, faster, faster, as fast as I could. To my right every so often I glimpsed a shadowy figure behind the skimpy branches of the trees. Someone not very tall. Mose? What did Mose want with me? Who *was* he? Why was he bothering me?

Within striking distance of the shed, I heard my name being called, vaguely, as if through mist. "Marylee! Marylee!"

I didn't turn around, instead I heaved the door open, and just as I fell inside the shed, I was grabbed from behind. Hard.

But I wouldn't give in easy. Whoever wanted to kill me was going to have a fight on his or her hands. I clawed and screamed, "Get away from me! What do you want from me?"

"Marylee! It's me."

Evan? I turned. It was Evan who'd grabbed me, and who held me now in his arms. I shrugged away from him, fright in my eyes. "It's you!" I said. "You were following me. It's been you all along. What do you want from me?"

"Marylee?" He let go of me slightly and I took that opportunity to back away from him. So it had been Evan all along! I backed away until I was flat against the rear of the shed, facing him, eyes wide. And suddenly all my doubts about Evan rose to the surface and bubbled there. Evan had had the picture of my parents all along. Evan's "specialty" was fires. Evan's sister was in prison for arson. Evan had conveniently disappeared for almost a week after our first date with no explanation. And don't even get me started on the fire in the gallery. Where had Evan been then? And Mose? No, again, I had trusted the wrong man.

Evan moved toward me and I shrank within myself.

"Marylee?" There was confusion in his eyes.

And then suddenly I was talking, telling him all the pent-up things that I'd carried around with me all these weeks. "You know something. I know you do. You know something about the fire, about the whole thing. Even Mose. I don't care what Jared said. I know it was Mose down there in front of my house. Who else would know about cameras the way he does? And you're protecting him, aren't you? And what about the picture of my parents? You said you didn't have one, so you needed mine. But you had one all along. And then there's the fire. You're protecting someone, I know it. Is it Mose? And you were there, weren't you, when my parents died in the fire? You were part of that gang of boys."

Evan ran his hand over his face, regarded me. "Marylee, you're talking crazy. You're not making any sense. Where are these ideas coming from?"

"They're coming from you, Evan, and there is so much you haven't told me from the very beginning. I just can't trust you."

He leaned against the wall of the shed opposite me and closed his eyes. When he spoke, his voice was low and hoarse. "And that kiss, that meant nothing to you?"

I stopped, clamped my mouth shut. It had meant a lot to me, of course it had. When he'd kissed me, my world had stopped and all the planets had cheered. But still, that hadn't done anything to get my questions answered. "It meant . . ." I paused. "It meant everything to me."

"Then how can you think I would hurt you?"

"But . . ." I stopped. "You chased me here. You grabbed me. You were behind the trees and following me." Even as I said it, I wondered. The person who had chased me had been smaller, more wiry. Someone like Mose. "You're protecting Mose," I said. "It was Mose who stood in the bus shelter looking up at the window of my apartment. It was Mose who was on the other side of the trees. Maybe he even followed us the other time."

"Mose?" He raised his eyebrows. "Marylee, nothing you have said in this crazy conversation has made any sense, but this is the craziest notion of them all."

I felt tired. I slumped down on a wooden bench that jutted out of the wall. It held. I sat there for a while thinking. "I came here because I thought this might be the place where the picture of my parents was taken. I just wanted to be sure." I looked at my surroundings for the first time. The shed was mostly empty. Long benches were built into two walls, and the only item not attached to the shed was a crusty, rusted outboard motor. I kicked at it with my foot. I could barely make out 4 HP along the side. One part of the casing was off and I looked through to the inner workings. My gaze was on the engine parts when I said, "It had to be Mose. I recognized him."

Evan shook his head. "It wasn't Mose. Mose is in Massachusetts with his family. But that would explain the police coming to the shop, then. He had no idea what that was all about."

"But what about the picture? You need to explain about the picture of my parents that you had all along. I saw it in your office. I saw it there."

Evan opened his eyes wide. "Marylee, I *told* you I was going to do that. Way back in the beginning when you first came to me with the picture, I told you I was going to digitize it, enlarge it and put them in various poses."

I looked at him and remembered. "Oh," I said. "But what about your sister? The one in prison for arson."

At the mention of his sister, he became very still, his hands in the pockets of his canvas coat. There was something unreadable in his eyes. And when he spoke, I barely heard his voice above the arrows of rain on the roof. "Why are you talking about my sister?"

"Because she may have been there. I know that the news said that witnesses reported seeing a woman fleeing from the hardware store when my parents were killed."

"And you, in some convoluted way, figured that that was my *sister?*"

I don't think I had ever seen him look so angry. I shrank away from him. "I heard there was a gang of boys who started random fires around the area. I heard that your older sister was the ringleader of the gang and that you were there when my parents' store burned down. That's why you recognized the picture of my parents when you looked at it the first time. It was because you recognized it. You need to tell me about your sister. You owe it to me."

"I don't owe you a thing, Marylee, but I'll tell you anyway if you promise to answer my questions." It seemed he could barely control his rage. I moved away from him. I suddenly found myself afraid of him, of everything. *Dear God,* I quietly prayed. *I need truth.*

He continued. "The only prison my sister is in is the prison of her own body. My sister has amyotrophic lateral sclerosis, ALS for short. She's in a nursing home, one not too far away from where my parents live."

I stared at him. The rain had momentarily stopped. The wet-wood smell of the shed made me catch my breath.

"Why didn't you tell me this?"

"I was respecting my sister's wishes. My sister is having difficulty with the whole diagnosis. She's trying to carry on as if everything is all right. She's asked us not to tell anyone about her condition."

"Oh." I felt deflated, awful and small. For a while I didn't say anything. There was nothing to say.

"Now," he said, moving toward me and sitting beside me on the bench. "You owe me some answers."

I was conscious of the closeness of him, the outdoor smell of his canvas jacket. He began, "What I would like to know is this — what ludicrous chain of thought processes were required to come to the conclusion that my sister had something to do with the fire in your parents' store?"

"Someone told me," I said simply.

"Someone who?"

"Martin Smythe, and Dot, his fiancée, confirmed it."

"Martin Smythe." He moved the word around on his tongue for a bit. "Good old Martin Smythe, whom we know is related to Danny Smythe, who worked for your parents and maybe was the one who helped himself from the cash register on a regular basis, that Martin Smythe."

I nodded.

"If someone is protecting someone, I would say that it's Martin Smythe, not me."

I just looked at him.

"Are you interested at all in why I came after you today? Why I wanted to find you? Why I chased after you in the rain? I called Johanna and she told me where you were. And I did see someone slinking around the bushes, but that wasn't me. And I've been worried about you since you told me about the camera. I've been trying to figure out that angle. I even talked to Jared."

"You did?"

He nodded. "And here's what I'm thinking. I'm thinking there might be more cash books, more proof, more information we need to find out about this so-called Danny Smythe. That's why I wanted to see you today. I wanted to see if there was more stuff that your aunt had, more books, maybe."

I didn't think I could answer him if I tried.

He took my hands between his own, said nothing.

"Evan," I said. "I'm sorry. I'm so sorry. I'm so sorry about your sister. I didn't mean . . ."

"I know." He rose and helped me up. "I came because I wanted to know if maybe there was more information here in Burlington. We need to get out of here while the rain has let up."

I nodded.

Outside, the wind had started and we made a dash through it up toward our cars. Warming up with a cup of coffee at the same café we'd been in just the previous week, he asked me if I'd ever been inside my childhood home.

I shook my head. I told him how I'd driven by, and the strange fear I'd felt. "But obviously I can't trust that fear." I looked down into my coffee. "There are other people living there now, I think a family with children. It's for sale."

"For sale? Maybe I should buy it. I'm looking for a place."

I shot him a glance.

Then he looked at his watch. "It's not too late. Maybe we could go there now."

We finished our coffees, and after I'd dropped my own car home, I got in Evan's and we drove toward the house where I grew up.

The fiercest part of the storm was over and now there was just a steady drizzle. He parked right in front of the house and turned the car off.

"What are we doing here?" I asked.

"We're looking for clues. Perhaps your parents left some boxes, anything. You never know."

"The chances of that . . ."

"I know. Slim to none. But we won't know until we try."

As we made our way up the cement walkway to the front, he pulled me close to him. That made me feel less afraid somehow, safe, maybe.

A thin young woman with a blond ponytail answered the bell. She looked tired when she said, "Yes?"

Evan introduced us and said that we were doing some research on the old house.

"Are you wanting to buy it?"

Evan said, "Possibly. But that's not exactly why we're here. I'm wondering if you would happen to know previous owners by the name of Samuels."

"That's not who we bought it from. We got it from someone named Johnson."

We stood on the porch in the rain. Evan ran his fingers through his hair like a comb and I realized where that cowlick came from, this habit he had of messing up his hair.

"May I ask how long you've lived here?"

"Around five years. My husband just got transferred out west. Is there anything else you'd like? I just got my children down to bed."

"Yes," Evan said. "I hate to impose, and perhaps today isn't the best day, but this is Marylee Simson and she lived here when she was a small child. We were wondering if we could have a look around the house. Or maybe we could come back when it's more convenient for you?"

She looked at us up and down and then said, "You might as well come in now. The kids will probably stay down."

We were a bit bedraggled, but we entered. She introduced herself as Patty Gettes. We followed her down a wide hallway. I felt as if I were meandering through a dream, and not quite getting my footing, as if I were staggering through pudding. In my mind I saw a tall woman with blond hair. I was being lifted into the air. I could almost hear the laughter. I wanted the three of us to stop, stand there until I got a handle on the dream.

She invited us into the kitchen, which didn't look familiar to me at all. She said, "We gutted this whole room when we moved in. Place was a disaster. Had to get all new appliances. Everything was old and falling apart."

I mostly listened as Evan engaged her in conversation about the house and what they'd done to change and upgrade it. All the upstairs bedrooms had been repainted but they'd left the wainscoting in the living room and the hallway was basically unchanged.

Evan said, "This place has an attic, right? Would there be any old boxes? That sort of thing? We're looking for some papers that may have belonged to the Samuelses."

She shook her head. In the distance a baby whimpered. She said, "Wait here. Let me just get Jamie. Looks like she's not down yet. I'll be right back."

When she left, Evan turned to me. "Is any of this familiar?"

"Some things. The hall mostly. But not in here."

"You said you have a recurring dream about mirrors?"

I nodded.

"Does anything about this house remind you of mirrors?"

Nothing did. But Gabby had said that the hardware store had been where the mirrors were. Yet why did I get a fleeting memory of mirrors when I'd driven past the backyard?

Patty came downstairs, a sleepy baby in her arms. She offered to take us through the rest of the house. "But what about your baby?" I asked.

"She'll be happy going on a bit of a walk, and by the time we're finished, she'll be ready to be put down again."

As we made our way upstairs, Evan said quietly to me, "See if any of the rooms generate a memory of those mirrors of yours."

I nodded.

Upstairs were three bedrooms. One, larger, was very obviously the master bedroom. It was messy with piles of clothing on the floor and an ironing board set up that looked like a repository for spare clothes rather than for ironing.

Since the children were asleep we didn't go into the two other bedrooms, only stood in the doorways of each. Something about the small bedroom next to the stairs seemed familiar and I stood there for a long time.

Evan took my hand. "Mirrors?" he asked.

I shook my head. "I'm not getting an impression of mirrors. It's something else."

"What?"

"I don't know," I said.

Meanwhile our hostess was going on and on about the renovation they'd done and how they'd planned so many, but now had to move.

"And this, this is a place we really wanted to fix up. It's a disaster." She took us down to the basement.

The entire lower level of the house was a cellar that contained heaps of old furniture, cardboard boxes, lamps, old shoes, boots and assorted pieces of toys.

We looked around. "Is any of this from the old owners?"

She shook her head. "It's all ours. Sad to say. A lot of it is my husband's mother's. She passed away and we inherited all her stuff, which is a lot of what you see. I know.

We have to go through it before we seriously think about moving."

I felt defeated, deflated. There was nothing here. We ascended the steps and as we did so, Patty said, "The one thing we didn't do since we moved in, and promised ourselves we would, was to fill in that old root cellar in the backyard."

I stopped where I was on the dusty steps. "What did you say?"

Patty and Evan looked at me, then Patty said, "The old root cellar in the backyard. It's unsafe. It's . . ." But she must've seen something in my look and she stopped. They both did.

Finally Evan cleared his throat and said, "Can we see this root cellar?"

"Sure. I don't even know how to get in, though. It's underneath some boards in the yard. I've only looked down there once. That was enough for me." She gave us flashlights and told us where to look.

The drizzle had let up, but it was still gray and everything was wet from the rain. Our boots and pant bottoms, dried finally from their first run-in with the rain, were drenched again.

After looking here and there and not finding anything but rain and weeds, Evan finally found the heavy piece of plywood that covered the entrance to the root cellar. It was nailed to a two-by-four and was heavy. We slid it aside. Craggy wooden steps led downstairs to a small bomb shelter–like concrete room. I'd been here before. I knew I had.

Rotten wooden shelves were on three sides. This would be the place that held home canning as well as produce like potatoes and carrots. Boards were piled against the third side, underneath the steps. Our flashlights cast eerie shadows on the wall. If I wasn't so intent on finding something, this is not the place I would ever venture by myself in the middle of a rainy evening. I was glad Evan was with me.

"What a place," Evan said, looking around him. "A great place, I should think, to store your veggies and things. But what a pain to get to from the main house."

The smell of the earth evoked a memory in me, waking up with dust in my nose and throat, and calling for my mother. But it wasn't my mother who came, it was Aunt Rose. At first glance the room looked empty, but I found mirrors stacked against one wall, then on a lower shelf, nearly buried by years of dirt, was a small mottled suitcase.

Evan placed the suitcase on one of the steps and opened it easily on its rusted-out hinges. It was filled with account books, similar to the ledger book that my aunt's lawyer had sent to me. Maybe this was nothing. Maybe this was merely where they'd stored old hardware-store records for the requisite seven years before destroying them, or maybe this was an important find. At the bottom of the suitcase was a large envelope full of snapshots. I flipped through these and felt a growing excitement. They were mostly ruined and moldy, but I recognized my parents, my mother and my father. There were pictures of this house, of a store, of them holding me. And while I carefully held the pictures, Evan had leaned against the ladder and was skimming the account books.

"I'd like to take these books with me," he said. "If the owners don't mind, that is. I'd like to compare these to the book that your aunt's lawyer sent. There might be something here."

I looked at the books he held, at the envelope of photos I had. "This is sure like what the lawyer sent, a ledger book along with photos."

The owner said we could take anything we wanted since the whole place was going to be filled in anyway. We thanked her and left.

When we arrived at my door he said that after I was inside, he wanted me to go to the balcony and wave so he would know everything was okay.

"I'll be fine," I said. "I've got a really good security system."

"Marylee! Someone got in and stole your chair."

"Point taken."

He walked me to my back door. When Evan turned to me, I expected him to say something. Instead, he reached for me, drew me to him and kissed me. Our embrace was long and tender.

"Now, do you still believe I'm trying to hurt you?"

I shook my head. "I think you've pretty well persuaded me to your point of view."

Seventeen

I know it was silly, but leaning over the balcony and waving at Evan, I thought about Romeo and Juliet. I half expected him to look up at me with puppy-dog eyes and launch into "But soft, what light in yonder window breaks?"

Instead, he blew me a kiss. How could I have ever doubted him? He honked as he drove out of the alley.

Even though it was quite late, I knew I wouldn't be able to sleep. So, true to form, I plugged in my kettle and got out a package of loose chamomile that Johanna had bought at a market for me.

I spread out all the new pictures on my kitchen table and tried to put them in order. Most were mildewed and the images on some of them were blurred beyond recognition. A few were stuck together and I could see that separating them would only destroy the images. I'd have to take them back to my shop and see if I could salvage them.

The pictures that I could make out, however, gave me a wealth of information about my parents. Finally I was looking at them after all these years. There was my mother seated on a couch, and me, a baby in her lap. There was another and another and another. There were a few of my mother and father standing in various poses in their hardware store.

As I looked at my mother, I began to see something else, too. I did look like her. There was a resemblance, if a slight one. I didn't have her long, full hair, nor her exquisite slenderness, but there was something about her eyes, her cheekbones that I saw in my own face when I looked in the mirror.

I drank my tea and went through the pictures one by one, over and over. I was anxious to know everything there was to know about them. So hungry was I for details that I didn't immediately hear the scratching sound. But when I did, my head jerked up. What was that? But then when it stopped, I wondered if it was something I'd only imagined. I went back to my pictures.

I found myself picking up a picture of a cat. "Scrapples." I said the name out loud. I didn't know where that name came from or how I knew it, but I did.

I heard the scratching sound again, followed by a high keening cry. The cat from the mystery bookstore across the way, most likely, I thought, but when I got up and walked to my front window, the bookstore was shut up tight and dark. No one was smoking down in the bus shelter. The street was empty. I went back to my kitchen and my parents.

I picked up a few pictures of people I didn't recognize. There were two of a man with thick horn-rimmed glasses and almost shoulder-length black hair underneath a fisherman's cap. Something about him was so familiar. I kept looking at him. And then at the cat. There were several more pictures of the man, and in one he stood next to my father. I closed my eyes. *Scrapples.* I could remember the cat, but why not the man? I lay my head on the kitchen table. I was so tired, yet I needed to know, needed to remember. This was important. Like the cat's name, I knew this was important, I just didn't know why. *Please, God, help me to remember.*

There was a man. He had a cookie for me. He took my hand. His hand was rough, cold. I was surprised at how cold his hand was. He put his finger to his lips and beckoned me to follow. I did. This was okay because he was a friend of Mommy and Daddy's. We walked outside following Scrapples. It was a sunny day. He took a handkerchief out of his pocket and wiped his forehead.

The memory faded. I opened my eyes, leaned my elbows on the table, my head in my hand. Then the sound of the cat again.

I woke up in the root cellar. There was damp earth all around me, but no matter how much I called, no one came. There were purple ribbons. I had my purple ribbons with me. But not the cat. Scrapples wasn't there.

I picked up the picture of the man with the glasses and the fisherman's cap. Suddenly it all became clear to me. I knew exactly who he was. I remembered him. I remembered his hands as he took the handkerchief out of his pocket. I have always liked looking at hands. He had asked about my quilts. But how would he know about my quilts if he'd never been in my apartment? None were yet displayed in my store.

I picked up the phone to call the police, but got no dial tone. Just what I need now, battery failed on the cordless. I scrambled through the pictures, through the tea leavings, but couldn't find my cell. Had I left it in Evan's car? No, most likely I'd left it downstairs in the store. I was always doing that. I needed to call the police about my suspicions. Quite possibly I should also call Evan. This was important.

I unlocked the door to my apartment and hurried down the back stairs. Had it always been this dark back here? That was my last thought before I felt pain and everything went black.

Gradually, gradually I began to see again. The first thing I noticed was that I was sitting in a chair, and that I was in the back room in my shop. My ankles were duct-taped together and my hands were duct-taped in my lap, tight together at the wrists. I tried to move them, but couldn't. The second thing I noticed was that I had one whopper of a headache. Number three was that I wasn't alone. Next to me someone else was duct-taped to a chair, but that person's mouth was covered with silver tape. I gasped when I saw who it was — Gabby! Each of her hands was taped to a chair arm and her legs were taped to the chair's legs.

Was my mouth duct-taped, too? I tried it. "Hey!" I shouted.

Good. My mouth wasn't taped. I would scream and scream until someone came.

Gabby jerked toward me. At about this time, my captor entered the room. He carried a red plastic jerrican of gasoline that sloshed at his side when he walked.

"I know who you are," I spat. "I know exactly who you are and what you did."

"Marybelle Samuels, I figured you would. Eventually. That's why I have to stop you."

"It was the quilts," I said to him. "At the craft fair you said I should sell my quilts at the fair. But how would you even know I quilted unless you'd been in my apartment and seen my quilting frame?"

"I regretted that the minute I said it. I worried you'd pick up on it right then. I was lucky. You didn't. But I knew you were getting close. It would only be a matter of time."

That had tipped me off, but there were other things, too. Physical things. The way he took the handkerchief out of his pocket, the way his hair bunched out under the woolen fisherman's cap he always wore. His hair used to be dark and long. It was now gray.

"You are Danny M. Smythe," I said. "Daniel Martin Smythe. You worked for my parents. And you killed them."

"No!" He slapped the jerrican down so hard on the floor that I could hear the gasoline splashing at the sides.

"But you did. You set that fire."

"No one was supposed to die. I just wanted the store to burn, the books destroyed. That's all that was supposed to happen."

"But they did die, which makes you a murderer."

"I knew the police wouldn't believe me, that it was an accident," Marty said. "But it was."

"You stole money from them and then killed them. It was no accident."

"It was an accident. It was! They weren't supposed to die. I begged your parents, I pleaded with them, but they wouldn't listen to me. They were going to go to the police, have me arrested. But I needed that money for the medical bills. For my wife." He was crouched next to his jerrican, a sad, pathetic little man. But then I realized, he was a sad, pathetic little man who had tied me and my aunt up with duct tape and had a can of gasoline and a book of matches.

He went on. "She was pregnant, my wife was, and there were complications. But the baby died. The stress of it . . ." He was talking, going on and on quietly. "If your parents paid me what I was worth, what I needed . . . If they hadn't gone all crazy when I had to take a few dollars here and there, they would be alive today. I wouldn't have had to do what I did."

"Murder them, you mean."

He glared at me. "It wasn't murder. They died accidentally in a fire that was just meant to destroy the proof, the books. How long do I have to keep telling you this?"

"But you could never be sure, could you, that the ledger books, along with my parents were destroyed. Rose told you, didn't she, that she had the books, that she knew what you'd done?"

He looked long at me, then unscrewed the cap of the jerrican, pulled out the yellow spout, turned it around, placed it on the opening and twisted the cap back on. Was he going to douse us with gasoline and light us on fire? I looked over at Gabby, whose eyes were wide above her taped mouth. I thought about the fire that had killed my parents. Is this what had happened to them? Had they been tied to chairs? The thought nauseated me. The news reports hadn't told me that. I thought about the fire in the art gallery. He had lit that one, too, I was sure of it.

I got the idea the reason he hadn't duct-taped my mouth was that after all these years he wanted to talk with me. Maybe that was part of it. If that was the case, I'd keep him talking. "Before you do what you're going to do, may I ask you a question?" I said. "How did you figure out who I was when *I* didn't even know who I was?"

"Simple. I've been watching. I've been waiting." While he talked, he poured gasoline into a shallow bowl he'd pulled out of his pocket. Was he making a bomb of some kind? "I knew you'd be back, the draw of family and all that. I knew how old you were. So, I just kept looking. If Rose had the books like she told me, I was sure she'd give them to you and that you would figure it out and come back. And if not, well I guess I'd have been just fine."

He set the gas can down on the floor and carefully unscrewed the cap and inverted the spout and set the cap back on. His movements were slow and precise. I said, "You put me down in the root cellar the day of the funeral. That was you, wasn't it? I remember that. Were you just going to leave me there? Kill me, too?"

"No! I'm not a murderer. I didn't kill anyone. I was desperate. I wouldn't have left you there to die. I would have come eventually. I was just using you as leverage, to get Rose to give me the accounts book."

"But obviously it didn't work, because you

never did get the book, did you?"

"No, my plan didn't work that day. That stupid cat gave you away before I had a chance to talk with Rose."

"Too bad. And then we left the next day."

He jerked his head up at me, and then back down at his work. In the center of the bowl of gasoline he placed a small chunky candle. I watched him, still trying to figure out what he was doing. He talked while he did this. "Rose called me a monster. I wasn't a monster. No one was supposed to die. It wasn't my fault. It was an accident. Rose double-crossed me. She left without giving me the book. No one knew where. Not even —" he looked toward Gabby "— family. I'm not a killer. Why won't anyone believe me?"

But even as he proclaimed to the world that he wasn't a killer, he unscrewed the jerrican again, reinserted the spout and added a bit more gas to the bowl. Next to me, Gabby was squirming and trying to speak through her taped mouth. My only recourse was to keep him talking, talking, talking.

"You disconnected the phone line upstairs," I said.

"I couldn't take any chances. My plan was to get this ready, then call you downstairs. You came down early. But no matter. We're now in Plan B."

"And all the stuff about Evan's childhood? You made all that up, right? To divert the attention away from yourself and onto an innocent person? I bought it. It almost worked."

"I knew it would. You'd just coming off having your heart broken. I made it my business to learn all about your failed engagement."

"And about his sister. You made that all up, too. I read the articles. Witnesses reported seeing a woman fleeing the scene. But that was you with your long hair, wasn't it?"

"People wore it long back then and so did I. It was just a stroke of luck that Evan has a sick sister."

"You set this whole thing up, the brush fire and the gang of boys. Did you recruit them?"

"I had nothing to do with them. There was a gang of boys who lit fires here and there and if you'd read further in the paper, you would've found out that the police found those boys and that they had nothing to do with the fire at the store."

"And Evan wasn't one of those boys."

"No. But you had that cozy little meeting at the shed earlier this evening. I figured that soon he'd persuade you over to his point of view."

"You followed me! It was you in the trees?"

"I had to. Both times. I had to keep an eye on you. You were getting too close."

He ignored me as he bent over his bomb or whatever it was he was making. Outside, a large truck rumbled down the road. I glanced toward it.

He said, "No one will come for you, if that's what you're thinking. It's too late at night."

"You should know something, Marty, before you set the place on fire. The books aren't here."

He wagged his finger at me. "That doesn't matter, does it? Because without your testimony, and the story of your childhood and Rose, I'll have nothing to worry about. On their own the books mean nothing. I'll be able to marry Dot and be happy for once in my life. With you gone, it'll all be over."

"You're wrong about that. You'll never get away with this." I scrambled for new topics to talk about. That was our only chance, to stall him. "And, and it was you, ah, you who set that fire in the gallery, too, didn't you?"

"You might say that fire is my specialty."

"And you got my car honking that night?"

"A bit of a tactical error on my part. I thought the books might be in your car. Mistakenly."

"And you planted the camera in my ceiling?"

"Of course."

"So you could get into my apartment on a regular basis, even when I changed the security code. And you called me that first time, asking for the security code. That was you!" How could I have been so stupid? "But, what about Dot?" I remembered the way she'd verified everything Marty had told me about Evan's family. "Is she in on this, too?"

He shook his head. "I convinced her. But leave Dot out of this. She's my only chance for happiness." He rummaged through my bolts of cloth. Then he grabbed a pair of new shears from one of my displays, tore them out of their package and began cutting long strips.

He'd cut maybe half a dozen when I asked, "What are you doing?"

"Never mind. By the time this place burns down I'll be long gone. Dot and me both. I have tickets." He patted his pocket. "For our honeymoon."

"Dot would never go with you if she knew what kind of a person you are."

He paused in his cutting and said, "That's why she'll never find out."

"But your first wife did find out, and that's why she left you."

He glared at me, and flung the scissors in my direction. I ducked and they missed me. He stood to full height and waved the handful of fabric strips. "No one was ever supposed to die! How many times do I have to keep saying this? I'm not a murderer! I liked your parents. They were good to me. It was just in this one thing they wouldn't budge. I had to do what I did. I had no choice in the matter!"

Carefully, he poured gasoline on each cloth piece, and placed one end of each strip in the bowl of gasoline, with the wet ends spread out like centipede legs.

I glared up at him and he glared down at me and I hated him. I hated him for what he'd done to me and my parents. I hated him for sending me and my aunt Rose away for twenty-eight years, twenty-eight years of running. He took my life away from me and I hated him for it. "But you killed them," I said. "And I will never forgive you for that."

Then he swung back and hit the side of my cheek with the back of his hand. Hard.

It brought new tears to my eyes and I felt things chattering inside my mouth. I tasted blood. I felt with my tongue, though, and all teeth seemed intact.

He turned away from me. "I loved my wife. She was all I had. You don't understand. She was all I had." He seemed near tears. "Just because I had no money."

The slap and his comment unleashed something deep inside of me. The tears I was feeling course down my cheeks had more to do with these new thoughts rather than any hurt or anger that I was feeling. Instead I began to feel something akin to pity. This poor little man had been wronged in life and thought he had no recourse but to lash out and kill things.

I remembered how Jesus responded to his captors, and even though I was worlds away from the kind of torment he endured, I, too, could learn something from the way he reacted. I prayed for wisdom. I began to understand that I didn't have to model Marty's behavior and copy him hatred for hatred. The rest of my life, even if it was only a few moments' duration, didn't need to be spent in revenge. "Marty," I said quietly. "You've suffered a lot. And I'm sorry for your loss, but don't you think enough people have died over this?"

He ignored me, climbed up my stepladder and placed the bowl with the wet gasoline-soaked rags and candle precariously on the top of a high shelf. He struck a match and lit the candle.

"This little interview is over," he said, climbing down. "I figure you have around twenty minutes before the candle burns into the gasoline, and the gasoline ignites the rags and your store goes up in flames. I'll be well across town by then. Ta-ta." He poured out the rest of the gasoline all over us and the floor and left.

"You can end it here," I called after him. "You can end this madness right here. You kill us and there is always going to be someone you have to kill. It will never end."

But he was gone.

Gabby implored me with her eyes.

"Pray!" I commanded to her. She nodded. I'd no doubt she'd been praying through this entire ordeal, anyway.

As I watched the candle burn, I knew we had to do something and had to do it fast. It's funny what goes through your mind at a time like this. I thought of my parents. I wanted to live because I didn't want to disappoint them. I wanted to make a go of it in this town so that they would be proud of me. I thought about Aunt Rose, who had given her life to keep me safe, and who'd taught me everything there was to know about crafts. I wanted this store to honor her legacy. I also thought about Evan, who was probably even now in his studio poring over the ledgers, comparing notes. I screamed and screamed until I was hoarse. I thought of the woman here beside me, Gabby, my new aunt. How could we die when we had so recently come to find each other?

"No!" I screamed. "This isn't going to happen."

Fortunately, my chair wasn't secured to the floor and I tried to rock it. Perhaps I could make it over to where the sharp mirror pieces were laid out on my student worktable. On my second rock all I managed to do was tip over my chair, hit my head hard on the floor, taste more blood. Tears of frustration welled in my eyes.

The candle was getting shorter. I could hear the wax sizzle as fragments of it fell into the gasoline. Marty had said twenty minutes, but the candle he had inserted seemed to be burning too quickly. If the candle had been on the table, I could merely blow it out, if I hadn't knocked over my chair. But of course, nothing is ever that easy.

Please, God. Please, God.

I swiveled the chair around and there on

the floor were the scissors Marty had thrown at me. Okay, Houdini, I told myself. Grab those scissors and get out of here. I scooted over until I was able to grasp them with the fingers of one hand. With my hands taped, it was impossible to cut the tape on my wrists, but I was able to hold the edge of the blade in one hand and cut away at the tape around my ankles.

Please, God. Please God. I was thankful, so thankful that this wasn't rope. To gnaw my way through rope would take forever. And with tape, once I had a fissure, the rest might be easy. I tried not to look at the candle. Gabby, I noticed, had been able to scoot her chair away from where the candle might fall, if the whole precarious homemade bomb toppled onto the floor.

I continued to scrape, up and down, up and down with the scissor blade. At one point, I cried out in pain as the edge cut my ankle rather than the tape. But if I didn't endure a bit of pain we would both die in here.

Finally, finally, it came loose. I leaned forward and hobbled over to Gabby. I cut the tape on her right wrist. "Quick," I said as I gave her the scissors. "Cut my hands free." She did.

"Yes!" I yelled, flexing my bloody wrists.

Then, as quickly as I could, I unwrapped my ankles and then undid the tape from Gabby's mouth and wrists and ankles and yelled, "Get that fire extinguisher." I pointed to where I kept one strapped to the wall near the door. She ran.

I grabbed my phone and climbed the step stool to try to blow the candle out. While I did so, I punched in Evan's number. He'd barely said hello before I said, "Evan? You need to come. You need to come! Call 911. I don't have time to explain."

Gabby ran in with the fire extinguisher and handed it to me. Just as I pulled the pin out, I heard a whoosh as the trailing fabric ends caught fire. Much to my happy surprise, a bowl of gasoline and some soaked rags are no match for a ten-pound fire extinguisher.

The place stank of gasoline, I stank of gasoline and there were white globules from the fire extinguisher all over everything in my store, but we were okay.

I climbed down from the step stool to where Gabby was sitting on the floor and shaking.

"We're okay," I said, cradling her. "We're okay. We're okay."

She said, "He's still out there. He'll come back. I should have realized that it wasn't

Evan on the phone asking me to come here. I should have known it was a trap. Then and there I should have called the police . . ." Her voice trailed off.

"It's okay."

"What if he's outside watching?"

"Evan's calling 911." Just to make sure, I punched in 911 myself.

Gabby said, "But Marty, of all people. He was so helpful at the funeral when your parents died. He even got up and spoke." She looked at me, her eyes wide. "Do you realize that? He got up at the funeral and told everybody how much he missed them and how good they were to work for. And when you went missing on the day of the funeral, he was there at the house and was so helpful in trying to find you. He said you'd taken off down the road chasing Scrapples, your cat. We never knew it was him. We wouldn't have dreamed it was him. We thought it was someone else, anyone but Marty."

"But Rose knew the truth," I said. "And she could tell no one because of the fear she felt for my life."

Gabby was weeping now. "If only she had. The police could have done something."

"She felt she had no choice."

We heard sirens and the front door burst

open and in two steps Evan was holding both of us, comforting us. And this was when all the fear and horror of what had just happened hit home, and I began to cry and shake. I just couldn't stop.

I was vaguely aware that my little shop was filling up with police officers and paramedics. Evan led Gabby and me to chairs in the coffee room, where he sat beside us and kept his arms around both of us and wouldn't let go.

Jared was there, and Nell, and they came and sat across from us and asked what had happened. Between the two of us, Gabby and me, we blubbered the story out.

Just when we thought we'd finished, Evan added, "I have some further information, Officers. I've spent the evening on the ledger books and found proof that Daniel Martin Smythe had been systematically embezzling funds from the hardware store. I have compiled figures. It looks like he'd taken upwards of ten thousand dollars before Adam Samuels figured this out. It was all there in the ledger books we found."

I had no idea it had been so much.

"I have also found some correspondence between Adam Samuels and Daniel Martin Smythe. The Samuelses were willing to negotiate, to keep this from becoming a police matter. They also offered to loan Martin money for the hospital bills. But when Martin repeatedly refused to make any effort to meet their terms, they told him they would be taking this to the police. That last correspondence is dated a day before the store burned down."

I asked, "Where did you find these letters?"

"In an envelope in the pages of the ledger book," he answered.

"And then he came back and wanted to destroy me." I looked around. "I could have lost everything," I said to Evan. "Everything."

"But you didn't," he said softly. "You didn't." And he held me closer than I'd ever been held by anyone before.

Epilogue

I carried an armful of daisies with me. My mother had loved daisies. Gabby told me that. She told me that when my parents were married, my mother had carried a huge bouquet of daisies. I know this, too, because I've seen the pictures. Evan helped digitize and enlarge several photographs of my parents, among them their wedding photos. My mother wore a simple white floor-length dress and also wore daisies in her long hair. When I'd commented on that, Gabby said, "Your mother always hated her hair. She always wanted it to be curlier. I remember her always saying that."

"Really?"

"You are very much like her. When you came to the door, it looked like Sonya was standing in front of me. That's why you gave me such a start. Except for the hair color, you are like her."

In their wedding pictures, my mother and

my father look happy as they stand under the daisy arbor and kiss for the cameras, oblivious of the storm that would change the course of their family just a few years down the road.

There were several photos of the daisy arbor, and many more of my parents and the entire family. I saw a young, pretty Rose as maid of honor. I looked at cousins and friends. I looked at a much younger Gabby with her husband Warren. There were others that Gabby pointed out in our sojourn through her numerous photo albums. I met grandparents and great-aunts and uncles who were now all dead, as well as lots of living cousins and aunts and uncles and family friends.

My knees were cold on the damp earth as I thought about all of this. They were simple stones, and stood side by side. Sonya Carol West Samuels and Adam James Samuels, and the dates of their births and deaths. I saw that my father was a year older than my mother. On my father's headstone were the words *Loved in life. Remembered Always.* On my mother's were the words *Remember the Moments, The Small Things.* Underneath this, a daisy was artfully carved.

It started to snow while I knelt there. Large flakes drifted lazily down and scattered on my coat, the grass and the daisies I'd lain across the ground in front of the headstones.

"I'm sorry," I said out loud. "I'm sorry it took me so long to get here. I love you both."

The night of the almost-fire in my shop, Evan had driven Gabby and me to the hospital. They'd wanted to check the cuts on my ankles, but especially my head. Since I'd been hit hard enough to knock me out, they had wanted to run all sorts of tests. I'd turned out fine. They'd also checked my cheek. Marty had really done a number on it when he'd hit me, and I'd probably have a bruise for a while. My teeth were all there and all intact, but there was one they wanted to keep an eye on in the weeks to come.

They only let me go that evening if I promised not to stay alone that night. When Gabby had offered to nurse me, I'd been more than happy to oblige.

The police had immediately gone to Marty's house, but he hadn't been there. They'd found my chair, however, which was taken down to the police station as part of the evidence.

There was an APB out on Daniel Martin Smythe, and the police had been confident that he'd be found before the night was over.

He wasn't.

They couldn't find him that night, nor the next day, nor the day after that. I went back to work, but decided to stay with Gabby at night until he was found. Evan came over almost every evening and I think Gabby liked having him around, having both of us around. She told us that cooking and making fancy meals for one wasn't nearly as fun as doing it for three. She was an excellent cook.

In the evenings after supper, the three of us would pore over her photo albums. I was hungry for details. Every picture was a new revelation, and behind every picture I wanted the long version of the story.

"That one." I would point. "It looks like this is some sort of fair? Or maybe a parade. I'm up on my father's shoulders? Where is this?"

"Oh, that . . ." And Gabby would lean back and chuckle in that soft way of hers. "That was in Rhode Island. You and your parents went there for a weekend when you were only two. They wanted you to see the parade. Do you see all those boats in the background? You went on a boat ride, apparently."

"What about this other picture? It looks

like they're all dressed up?"

"That was for Uncle Lon's funeral, your great-uncle on your mother's side. What an eccentric old geezer he was, grouchy as all get out, never married, your typical grumpy old man. Yet when he died, we all missed him. Still do. He could tell stories, boy could he tell the tales."

"Tell me some of them," I implored.

And she did.

We moved through book after book this way. I found a number of pictures that I wanted duplicates of, and Evan did this for me.

We also solved the mystery of the magazine picture. That picture of my parents at the lake had been taken the day they'd become engaged. It had ended up as an engagement announcement in a small weekly newspaper that was delivered free to Burlington homes. Someone from a women's magazine had seen the picture, liked it, and had ended up getting the rights to use it in his magazine as an illustration for a short story.

But still Marty remained at large.

Sometimes people from the church came by. Johanna brought flowers and a bagful of romance novels for me to read. She stayed for supper one night and the four of us, Johanna, Gabby, Evan and I, ended up playing dominoes until late. Later at the door, Johanna told me, "My prayers have been answered."

"What do you mean?"

"I prayed that Evan would get past that thick hedge of his soul, and it looks like that has happened." And then she hugged me.

The fall sale in my store came and went, and of course, Barbara was a big help. Christmas, too, was a smashing success and I exceeded all sales records.

But still Martin Smythe had not been found.

Dot, of course, was heartbroken when she learned about the type of man Marty was, and I felt sorry for her and brought her a cake and sat with her. Weeks passed. It worried me, but short of hiding out in Gabby's house, there was not a lot I could do. I refused to let Martin have this much control over my life.

I could hear the gentle breeze in the trees and I smelled the snow now as it fell, coating the place where I knelt like powdered sugar. After a few minutes, I stood and dusted off my coat. Under a tree, some distance away, Evan sat on a bench. He wanted to give me privacy, he'd said, on this, my first visit to my parents' graves. I headed toward him and was surprised to see him leaning forward, his elbows on his knees, bent into his cell phone.

As I got closer, I caught the edges of his conversation. "Okay, then," he said. "That's really good news. Yeah. Thanks. Thanks for letting me know. I'll be sure to tell her."

He snapped his phone closed when I got there. "That was Jared," he said. "They finally found Marty. They've arrested him. They're bringing him in. He was hiding out in a cabin in the backwoods of Maine."

I stared at him. For a moment I couldn't move. "It's over then," I said quietly. "It's finally over."

"It's not over." He held out his hands, and when I took them he pulled me close and said, "It's just beginning."

And then he winked.

Dear Reader

I live in a part of the world where roots and a sense of home are very important. One of the first questions that people in my neck of the woods ask is, “So where are you from?” But, because I come from a family that moved around a lot, I never quite know how to answer.

My husband and I have lived in three countries, and even now when I go to visit my mother’s home, I am not going home because my parents moved to that place well after I was married. The fact that I have no roots used to be very distressing to me. I was jealous of individuals who could trace their families back through the generations, who had a sense of clan and family and place, who had to rent campgrounds to have family reunions. I’ve never had that. I have never felt like I quite belonged in all the places I’ve lived.

Marylee in *Shadows in the Mirror* struggles with more than just a lack of roots. She was raised by a single aunt, and never told anything about her family. As she struggles toward identity, she struggles to come to know what's important in life.

Some years ago my attention was drawn to Psalm 90:1, "Lord you have been *my* dwelling place in all generations." This verse just jumped out of the page at me and I began to realize that God doesn't *provide* me with a home, he *is* my home. He is my dwelling place.

I hope you enjoy this first book in my new SHADOWS series. I invite you to visit my Web site: www.writerhall.com.

Linda Hall

QUESTIONS FOR DISCUSSION

1. Marylee lacked a sense of home. Do you ever feel this way? What can you do about this?

2. Do you think it's possible to feel this way even if you do know where you come from? Why?

3. Marylee moved to a town where she knew no one in order to find out the truth about her family. It was a difficult task. In what ways have you done something difficult in order to put something right?

4. Growing up with her aunt, Marylee always felt different. What was your own "growing up" family like? Did you always feel as if you fit in, or did you ever feel you didn't belong? Why or why not?

5. Rose, the aunt who raised her, didn't tell

Marylee anything about her childhood. Do you think she was justified in doing this? How would you have handled the situation if you were Rose?

6. What values did Aunt Rose instill in Marylee? Do you think she was a good parent? Why or why not?

7. Marylee makes assumptions about Evan based on false information. Have you ever judged someone in this manner? How did you make amends?

8. Marylee's best friend, Johanna, has lots of close family members, yet she takes Marylee under her wing, even inviting her for a family Christmas. Is there someone in your sphere of influence to whom you might need to show some extra love? What can you do for the Marylees in your church group?

9. The villain was convinced his actions were justified. In what ways do we justify our own, more minor, bad actions? What advice would you give to someone in a similar situation?

10. What did Marylee discover at the end?

What did she discover about her inner strengths?

ABOUT THE AUTHOR

When people ask award-winning author **Linda Hall** when it was that she got the bug for writing, she answers that she was probably born with a pencil in her hand. Linda has always loved reading and would read far into the night, way past when she was supposed to turn her lights out. She still enjoys reading and probably reads a novel a week.

She also loved to write, and she drove her childhood friends crazy, wanting to spend summer afternoons making up group stories. She's carried that love into adulthood with twelve novels.

Linda has been married for thirty-five years to a wonderful and supportive husband, who reads everything she writes and who is always her first editor. The Halls have two children and three grandchildren.

Growing up in New Jersey, she took many trips to the shore where her love of the ocean was nurtured. When she's not writing, she and her husband enjoy sailing the St. John River system and the coast of Maine in their twenty-eight-foot sailboat, *Gypsy Rover II.*

Linda loves to hear from her readers and can be contacted at Linda@writerhall.com. She invites her readers to her Web site, which includes her blog and pictures of her sailboat: www.writerhall.com.

The employees of Thorndike Press hope you have enjoyed this Large Print book. All our Thorndike and Wheeler Large Print titles are designed for easy reading, and all our books are made to last. Other Thorndike Press Large Print books are available at your library, through selected bookstores, or directly from us.

For information about titles, please call:

(800) 223-1244

or visit our Web site at:

http://gale.cengage.com/thorndike

To share your comments, please write:

Publisher
Thorndike Press
295 Kennedy Memorial Drive
Waterville, ME 04901